An Unk

Ananya Mukherjee is a former business journalist and the ex-editor of *HRM Asia*, a leading business title in the Asia-Pacific region. She is an acclaimed writer with more than 1000 publications to her credit. Before moving to Singapore, she had amassed years of experience in Indian print and television media. Her journalistic acumen covers a whole gamut of subjects, including politics, lifestyle and business.

Ardh-Satya & Other Stories, Ananya's first book, is a collection of twenty short stories and was published in 2016. It has received rave reviews from Indian and international media. *Ardh-Satya*, an adaptation from the title story, was staged at Dastak, a Hindi Theatre Festival in Singapore and at the prestigious Kala Ghoda festival in Mumbai, India.

Ananya also writes poetry in Hindi. Six of her poems were recently published in a literary magazine, *Nazariya*, in India. In addition, Ananya writes scripts in Bengali for audio plays. Her recent work, *Madhumashe* and *Ontoreen*, were staged by stalwarts of the entertainment industry in Kolkata in 2020. She has also acted in a very popular short film, *Ilish*, released in 2021.

A theatre artiste, avid traveller, trained dancer and show anchor, she is a known figure in the cultural and literary circles in Singapore and India.

Ananya also wears a senior corporate leadership hat and leads global communications in Asia and Europe for a US-based multinational company.

An Unborn Desire

Ananya Mukherjee

Hi Rishi,
Hope you enjoy
reading the book!

Best wishes,
Ananya Mukherjee
Jan 2023

RUPA

Published by
Rupa Publications India Pvt. Ltd 2021
7/16, Ansari Road, Daryaganj
New Delhi 110002

Sales centres:
Allahabad Bengaluru Chennai
Hyderabad Jaipur Kathmandu
Kolkata Mumbai

Copyright © Ananya Mukherjee 2021

ISBN: 978-93-91256-20-3

First impression 2021

10 9 8 7 6 5 4 3 2 1

The moral right of the authors has been asserted.

Printed at HT Media Ltd, Greater Noida

To Swarup and Sampoorna.
My most precious ones.
Sometimes you search for treasures and find nothing;
sometimes, you search for nothing and find treasures.
A miracle happens when you set out for a treasure hunt without
a map and find a world of wealth waiting for you.
Thank you for being mine.

Contents

Of Stars, Planets and Boundaries

What are you writing?
A memoir.
Of what? Life?
Of memories. Of stories—half-forgotten and fully lived.

Of people—dead, living and the living dead,
within and without me.
And of love.

Preface

Songs are but poems that have never been read.
And what about the songs that haven't been heard?
They become stories.
And what about the stories that were never told?
They become memories ... perhaps.
And what happens to memories that are buried?
On rainy nights such as these, they float through the universe as clouds
And lyrically settle into a deep sigh.

When I listen to your voice, all I hear is gurgling laughter, waiting to brim over and infect me. When I see you in your silence, all I read are the songs you have hidden in your eyes. Your touch is almost melodic, like the opening stanza of a couplet, rhythmic yet secretive. Sometimes in unrehearsed moments of solitude and tranquillity, I remember the fragrance of a perfume and I know you are there. And in that momentous juncture, when all my senses surrender and I hold my muted soul in silence, you reach out to me.

That's where we begin to connect.

This book is an attempt to weave observation and imagination seamlessly into a single fabric, to tell your stories through my voice. I earnestly hope some of it will strike a chord with you.

Warm regards

Unborn Desires

I knocked on a closed door.
A part of me welcomed me in.
Then I opened the window wide and let another part of me fly out...

Unborn Desires

Do you know what they did to me?

No, I don't.

Of course, you don't! How could you? You were sedated and lying there like a rag doll. Unconscious. While they cut me up into little pieces with cold metal, severing me from you forever.

I am sorry. I didn't know you suffered as I did. Did it hurt? They convinced me you wouldn't feel a thing. You weren't human yet.

Oh, my body—or whatever that piece of flesh and blood was—felt nothing. Just a pinch. A tiny pinch of the cold sterilised weapon. But my soul ...

Your soul? What about your soul?

Yes, my formless, my infinite, my liberated soul. It was there within that clot of flesh. It was living and breathing within your boundaries. One day I will find a body again and take form. Would you recognise me then, Mamma?

'Did you sleep at all on the flight?' Kiara asked Kabir, rubbing her eyes.

'Yeah, kind of. I woke up every now and then. It

was a bumpy ride. What about you?' Kabir questioned, looking at her in wonder. How could such a stunningly beautiful and intelligent grown-up woman in her mid-forties rub her eyes like a child! Even with her large floating eyes half covered by her fists, one could easily see that she was gorgeous. The fifteen years between him and Kiara were not immediately obvious to onlookers simply because of the way Kiara kept herself young— both physically and psychologically, something that attracted Kabir to Kiara the most.

'Not much. I hope to catch a nap in the afternoon after we reach home,' Kiara replied settling her bag and jacket into the chair.

'Yes, do that. It's going to be a long night.' Kabir winked and continued, 'Are you hungry?'

'Just a little. Shall we order some breakfast?'

'Good idea. I am in no mood to eat on the flight back. Does your mum know we will be home this afternoon?' Kabir asked.

'Yes, I spoke to her the day before and have asked her to send the maid to clean the house and get some groceries. She mentioned something about the air conditioner in one of the bedrooms not working well.'

'Sure, love. Will get that fixed,' he said, reaching out for her hand, gently caressing the fingers and stopping to admire the ring for the umpteenth time. It had a brilliant round, perfectly cut, large diamond with a cluster of smaller diamonds around the circumference, set against a gold band. The 'rock' had been a hit ever since they first saw it. 'Whoever chose that for you has very good taste, I must say.'

Kiara smiled, brushing the hair falling on her face. 'Yes, he is a man of fine taste. He has chosen me.' They both laughed at that very usual private joke. 'Jokes apart, it's a beautiful ring. Thank you, baby.' She raised his hand and kissed it lightly.

They were sitting together for breakfast at their usual two-seater table near the A-gate at the first-class lounge in Dubai International Airport. They saw themselves as creatures of habit and their menu seldom veered from their careful routine. Eggs benedict, green apple juice for Kiara and for Kabir an egg white omelette with onions, chillies and tomatoes, crispy fried bacon, a hash brown, orange juice and brown toasts on the side, to be followed by a pot of Darjeeling tea and a double espresso with hot milk on the side. The occasional indulgence appeared in the shape of a warm waffle with a drizzle of honey. That was always meant to be shared.

'How much time do we have? I want to have a look at some watches,' Kiara said while pouring honey over a piece of the waffle.

'Oh, we have about an hour before we board. Do you have something specific in mind?' Kabir asked.

'I saw a Tissot with a dark red leather band and a white dial. I quite like it, but I am not sure if it's the right shape for my broad wrist.'

'I know the one you are talking about. I thought it looked too dainty and too feminine for your personality.'

'What is that supposed to mean? Are you telling me that I am the aggressive-alpha-male-dominating type?'

'You bet, Ms ENTJ!' Kabir responded with a sheepish grin, 'Even your psychoanalysis test confirms. A "born leader" in other words means alpha. Can't you see how henpecked I am?' They broke into a wild bout of giggles, unmindful of the heads that turned towards them. It wasn't common for travellers in posh business class lounges such as this one to speak or laugh out so loud.

After breakfast, they walked around the aisles full of brands of chocolate, perfumes, duty-free liquor, sunglasses, watches, electronic and gold shops, in vain. Not finding what they were looking for, they decided to walk back to the gate and wait for the boarding call.

'I don't like this airport. It feels like I am trying to catch a flight in a shopping mall,' Kiara said while looking at the crowd swarming around her. There were men and women and children everywhere, noisily rushing out through the elevators, standing on every step of the long stretch of the escalators, in queues in front of washrooms and lined up at every coffee shop. It was a busy transit point.

'Don't bother! Let's go to the quieter zone and wait near the gate,' Kabir said, noting her discomfort.

She looked at him with a little hint of admiration. *'How I love this unaffected-by-the-world-yet-comforting-to-the-ones-I-care-for nature that seldom feels distracted by all that could be negative,'* she thought to herself.

'Petrichor, hiraeth and timshel are my three favourite words. What are yours?' she asked him once they had moved to another section of the airport.

'Beautiful words. Explain their meanings to me again, please.'

Kiara smiled. 'Petrichor is the way the earth smells after the first rains; hiraeth is the longing to be home and timshel means "thou mayest"—in other words, we always have the choice of good over evil.'

'Oh, I recall this. You told me what petrichor meant while we were in Istanbul. I think you spoke about timshel in Cape Town.'

'Okay, so I planted a word in your mind in different cities and you will now remember them whenever you travel back in time. Tell me about your favourite words,' Kiara insisted.

'Do the words have to be as exotic as yours?' Kabir asked.

'Not at all. Just as exotic as you.' She smiled.

'Okay … mine are courage, faith and magic.'

'How lovely! I love magic too. It puts the twinkle back in my eyes.'

'That's what the fairy godmother said Cinderella would ever need in her life.'

Their conversation was cut short by the boarding call for passengers flying to Singapore. The couple was heading back to Singapore from London. They had been living together—as partners—for over two years now. Kiara had flown to London for a business conference, and Kabir had decided to take a few days off to be with her. The tail end of her business trip had become a holiday. It was their fifth trip to London together in the last two years, but they both thought that they could never outgrow the city and its charms. Their four-day extended weekend had been packed with activities: two musicals, a few trips to Regent Street and Oxford Street, long walks by the Thames, hot chocolate and random hours at pubs in Borough Market.

Sonia, Kiara's mum, lived a couple of blocks away from the sea-facing condominium that Kabir and Kiara shared in Singapore. She lived alone after Kiara's father passed away, working in her quiet home. She was a therapist who treated her clients through the method of past life regression using hypnotic trance techniques.

Kiara was her only child; instead of being picky and protective about the man Kiara had chosen for herself, she had preferred to keep her own opinions of the 'young boy' under a tight leash. Though she was initially perturbed by the stark age gap between Kiara and Kabir, she wanted to focus on the joy the relationship brought to her daughter.

'Mum,' Kabir began at the dinner table set to welcome them home at Sonia's place. 'How much of these techniques are true and what percentage is left to the client's imagination … or your interpretation?' He loved poking her and teasing her. Kiara smiled as her mum explained calmly.

'See, Kabir, I am not a fraud, if that's what you mean. There have been a considerable number of cases where people have recalled information that I have subsequently verified with sources. People who personally knew who they were in their past lives.' Sonia was calm, and was trying her best to not be irritated by Kabir's impertinence.

'You mean someone walks through that door and you immediately know who he was in his past life? That must be fun—like an X-ray of your past résumé! You could be a king, a politician or just a nobody today. But behold, in your past life you were a bleeding and dying soldier in a war or a sorceress being burnt alive or maybe even a princess, gaily picking cherries in an orchard! Wow! This is like a social media game,' Kabir continued in his characteristic humour, his words teasing and laced with sarcasm.

'Kabir, stop bothering Mum,' Kiara reprimanded with an affectionate tap on his hand.

By now, Sonia was beginning to lose her patience. She cleared her throat and decided to explain the mechanism of the technique.

'The concept, rather the fact that we have past lives is

increasingly accepted by a significant number of people across the world. When clients are hypnotised to a certain level—and I, being a professional, know what that level is—they can recall their past lives. Deeper than that, what we call soul memories rise up to their conscious awareness. It is at this stage that people recall their deaths.'

The conversation had taken an interesting turn and even Kabir who had initiated the discussion in a jest now began to get curious.

'What if people have bad memories of their deaths?'

'If the death has been traumatic, we provide counselling and therapy.'

'And do they really remember how they died or the people around them? What do they see?'

'Well,' Sonia responded with a contented grin, 'it varies from person to person. Most clients share that they see themselves floating out of their physical bodies, or into a tunnel of darkness with a white light at the end. They describe a strong force sucking them out of it, then a sudden sense of lightness and freedom. Some even recall the scene of their own death with a distinctive sense of detachment.'

'What if the therapist prompts or directs these answers?'

'When in deep hypnosis, a client responds to questions extremely literally. In other words, the client will only respond directly to a given question. The scope for deliberate falsification of information is virtually impossible unless the client is not really in a deep trance. A skilled therapist can tell when he or she is faking it. A person in a regression cannot just be directed to experience something unless they already possess the information to respond. What he or she is sharing is a true inter-life soul memory,' Sonia elaborated.

'So ... you mean ... the soul never forgets, no matter how different the new body is?'

'Yes, that is true!'

'Wow! Does that imply that anyone could actually—of course, under the supervision of a professional therapist—revisit his past and discover mysteries or truths about his life and death?'

'Yes, if they want to.'

'Including people like me? I mean people who have no troubling recurrent nightmares or visions to suggest that they may have had a traumatic past?'

'Absolutely!'

Kabir's eyes grew brighter with every new question. It started to make Kiara nervous. *What was he thinking?* Kiara had full faith in her mother's potential as a therapist and she knew that her mother had helped countless others, but she wasn't keen to experiment. She had never had a session and she didn't want Kabir to either. These were things you didn't want to explore at home.

But Kiara's suspicions were founded.

'Can I take a test?' Kabir asked Sonia abruptly. 'Don't get me wrong, Mum. I am not challenging you, I'm just curious.'

'Kabir ... no!' Kiara immediately put her foot down.

'Please, Kiara—'

'How childish can you be! This isn't a DNA test. You don't need this in your life,' she snapped, realising that this had already gone too far for her comfort.

'—please, Mum! I want to know who I was, what my past life looked and felt like! Don't you worry, you will soon discover you are actually living with a prince', he joked, and winked at Kiara.

'Please stop! *I* don't want to know and I am not sure why you would subject yourself to the memory of a life you don't connect with. You don't even believe in this. Come on, Kabir! There's nothing earth shattering about knowing who you were in your last birth. How does it matter?'

Oh Kiara! Don't suck the fun out of this. Please! said with said 'I am just curious and I want to know who I was. I think I have the right to that information. If Mum refuses on your behalf, I am sure there are other therapists in Singapore who can answer my questions,' Kabir said adamantly.

After much pleading, Sonia agreed to a session with Kabir, but only on one condition. Kiara would be allowed to watch, as a silent witness to the act.

Sonia's therapy chamber was sparse: a simple neat room in white with only a table, two plastic chairs and a sleek lamp. It was nothing like Whoopie Goldberg's den in *The Ghost*, something Kabir had imagined in great detail. There was a flip chart next to the table and a white board with some markers next to it. A single glass window shone light into the room, but it was shut tight. On the table were insignificant little objects: marble balls, stick pads, a pen and two glasses of water.

Sonia gestured gestured for Kabir, asking him to sit on a chair and relax. She pointed at another chair away from them for Kiara. Then she sat on the table, facing Kabir.

Kiara saw the gradual changes. Kabir was slowly moving into a state of trance as her mum practised her usual hypnotism routine. Then, suddenly, the energy in the room shifted. Kabir began to sink deeper and deeper into himself. Slowly and deeply, she began to feel the distance between their consciousness widening. Kiara imagined a growing chasm. She looked at her mother's poise and could sense that Kabir was now ready.

'Can you hear me?' Sonia asked quietly.

'Yes,' Kabir replied in a monotone, 'I can hear you.'

'What do you see?'

'Darkness.'

'Does it have a form? Describe what you see.'

'Yes, it has form. It's like a tube—soft, wet and a bit slimy.'

'Where are you in this tube?'

'I can't see myself ... but I can feel it. I am right in the middle. Embedded on the dark bulb.'

'And? What's happening around you?'

'Something sharp. I can see it. A cold metal knife-like thing ... it's slicing through a wall. Oh. It's tearing me apart ... ripping me away ... from that soft wet cushion. Scooping out bits of me. There is something hot. Blood all over. I am dripping with blood. Aaah ... it's too much pain. It's terrible.'

'Unusual! You still don't see yourself?'

'No. I don't see a definite form, but I recognise myself. I am a lump of flesh.'

'How big?'

'Tiny. Only a few centimetres ... maybe.'

'What other things are happening?'

'Stillness now. Just a light, quiet stillness somehow. I don't feel any pain any more. Wait ... I can see some lights, like dots on a green curtain. There is some sunshine too. Very bright. A man and a woman are dressed in white lab coats. It looks like a hospital.'

'What are they saying?'

The man is saying, "It's over." "It's over. Don't worry. We will let you rest for a while. Then you can go home."'

'Are they talking to you?'

'No, not to me!'

'Who are they talking to?'

'It's a ... young girl. She is covered in a green sheet; she's holding it up to her chest. She looks tired and very scared. Curly hair, deep sunken eyes, a little cleft in the chin. She's crying ... hold on. Oh!'

'What?'

'Oh wait ... I know that face. Oh, I know it so well, so close ... it's ... it's Kiara!'

In another part of the room, Kiara sat motionless, digging her nails into her palms as tears flooded her eyes. Her vision blurred as she remembered that dingy hospital room with its green curtains. She recalled her teenage accident—the only dark secret she had kept from the world—the termination of a lump of flesh from her womb.

Three Sides of a Coin

You appear
like a confession from my soul.
The fragrance of a tropical breeze, soon after the first
monsoon shower
Calming, yet expectant.

Your promises resonate
Like church bells in an abandoned monastery—
hollow in its heaviness, yet barren.

Your words evoke a forgotten melody,
Like an innocent lullaby,
crippled without a tune and the memory of sleep …
Conjuring up nothingness out of nothingness.

The paradoxical completion of an untold story.

Cape Town, South Africa

There is something so perfectly unsynchronised about this moment. It refuses rhythm or pattern. It is as if a detracted second has unceremoniously fallen out of the hands of a clock.

It is a missed sound in a beat of familiar integers.

And, in this undecorated time frame of lost coordinates, I realise that it is my head that feels heavy. In fact, very heavy! The temples are throbbing again, the dull ache is back and I am clueless as to where I am.

Is the surgery over or am I still under the influence of anaesthesia?

They said it was a complicated process, that the operation could take hours. The tumour is larger than usual and life threatening at this stage. I had mustered the courage to ask if there were chances of a cognitive dysfunction or a behavioural impairment after the operation. My surgeon had replied in a voice as cold and dispassionate as the knife. He dutifully informed me that I had crossed the mark. 'I don't wish to mislead you. It is a moment between life and death now. You could wake up to a new day and walk out of this like you were never here or you could—'

'Or I could fall into a timeless slumber, never to see the clouds cascading down the Table Mountains or the sun-kissed Indian Ocean crashing against the boulders in the southern tip of the majestic African continent.' I interrupted.

'Unfortunately, life is neither as romantic nor as poetic as you portray it to be.' He had smiled gently. I knew he was just being polite. They had to be nice to dying patients.

I am thirsty and restless. There is a half-full glass of water on the bedside table; I wonder if it's a metaphor. I cannot remember when I drank the other half, or if the tumbler belongs to someone else. I pull myself upright with some effort and pour the stale liquid down my throat. It has a strange metallic taste. I look around to check the date and time. There are no calendars but the digital table clock has stopped at seventeen past five. From the light streaming through the glass ocean-facing panel, I can gauge that it is close to noon. The ocean is beginning to sound hoarse, as if angry and impatient for the high tide. The waves bellow in a frenzy, like a dervish swept up in the heightened ecstasy of a trance.

I look around the room. Everything is painted in either white or in shades of aquatic blue. The bed, the walls and the little bean bag facing the glass window with their soothing minty blue somewhat calm my anxiousness.

Wait—

I can hear voices in the floor below.

So, I am not alone. There are people here keeping me company. I try hard to identify the voices or catch a few words, but they are speaking in low whispers.

'Are you not taking me to the hospital soon? You know it's an emergency, then why are we delaying it for nothing? And what on earth am I doing in a blue beach house in Cape Town of all places when I should be in an operation theatre getting rid of a piece of flesh that has trespassed into the territories of my mind? Something is terribly wrong. I have to be elsewhere.' I want to scream my questions, but I find no voice.

Concurrently, a rationale is contradicting my logic and telling me: *'No, I have to be here now. The coordinates are right, and I would soon find out the axes too.'*

The door opens and Menaka steps in. I don't recognise her at first. Her skin is a lot lighter than I remember. Her hair lit with shades of copper and brown. A sharp little nose sits pretty on her face. No make-up as usual, just a fine line of kohl around her large floating eyes and a hint of a nude lipstick. She looks a bit tired, but seems as confident as ever. Dressed in a white cotton dress, Menaka's lean frame reveals the contours of a dancer.

She walks straight into the room, without noticing or acknowledging my presence. She heads to the glass panel and faces the raging ocean. I can only see her back from where I lie in my bed.

I have to admit, there is an aura about her—much like the nymph or *apsara* she is named after. The rich arrogance of an artiste! I admire her from a distance but do not call out. After having spent a few minutes admiring the blueness of the ocean, she finally turns towards me.

'So?'

'So, what?'

'Are you happy to see me?'

'Honestly? I am surprised to see you here.'

'Ditto. I hadn't really thought I would make it so far as to look you up.'

'So, what brings you here?'

'I need to settle some scores.'

'No, Menaka. Please don't start this all over again. Can you not see I am ill?'

'Yes, I can see you the way you are. But if not now, when? When will you get any better?'

I understand exactly what she means.

'Fine ... go on ...'

I give up, but before she starts, I offer her an apology. 'Look, I am sorry, I know you have done well in life ... and I know you could have done much better had I supported you. But I was too young and I did not have the confidence to stand up for you—'

'Oh, cut that crap,' she interrupts. 'You never believed in my potential. You backed off when I needed you most.'

I can see her smirk complementing the accusation. Menaka reaches out to touch my hand. It's cold, like a steel knife being tested for its sharpness. I shiver under the ruthlessness and turn away to swallow the bitterness rising from the pit of my stomach.

What on earth does she mean? Why is she here if all she wants is to pour her venom into me with that single touch?

But I also understand. Menaka is an artiste. She can seem haughty, but she's a committed theatre actor and a trained dancer. I remember her on stage—she is a dream. A popular director had once said to her, 'A painting comes to life when you are on stage,' I agree. Needless to say, she is very popular with men, always sought after, but I know how little she respects them or the relationships they offer.

Menaka and my worlds are different; our attitudes, values, upbringing ... everything is different. She is never humble, and I have little appreciation for her arrogance. I don't know how our paths first crossed, and fortunately they have never met. We are too different to be put into the same basket, in love or in friendship, and we have always trampled over each other's egos and pride at odd junctures, confronted each other in ugly warfare and left each other's presence with a bad taste lingering in our mouths. I never found out why she hates my ordinariness, but the feeling has been mutual. Her visit this afternoon only reinstates that distaste.

'Why are you here?' I decide to confront her cold gaze.

'I had to see you dead for myself, bitch,' Menaka replies with a mocking smile. This is the first time in many years that she calls me by that name, a word she would use when we were friends. 'Besides, I have to tell you a story,' she continues.

'What a time for storytelling! Go on.'

'There's never a good time for this story. Do you remember when we were in high school, and a rather popular cosmetic brand had offered you a modelling assignment?'

'Yes, how can I ever forget!' It took me back. I sighed wistfully. 'Dad refused on my behalf and of course, that was the end of it. I didn't even get to respond to the agency. But what's that got to do with anything?' I wonder why she is bringing this up after so many years have passed. Is she trying to remind me of a failed dream?

'I took that assignment. I found the address of the agency that had approached you, contacted them and said you weren't willing, but I was. They took me in for a trial and I did fine, I think. I was not sure I would get the contract. So, I did what I could ...' She winks.

'What does that mean?'

'I slept with the casting agent. Gosh! I was so desperate to sign that contract and get that break I would have done anything.'

'I don't believe it!'

'You have to believe the truth. Anyway, I got the contract and my face was launched in the world of glamour while you...'

'Well ... I would never ever sleep with anyone to get a job.'

'Of course, you would not! That's why you are where you are.' Her shameless arrogance reaches another pitch and it begins to grate on me.

'So, you travelled half way across the world to tell me that you stole an offer that was originally meant for me, then slept with the agent to make it happen, and now you are a celebrity and I am not? What's the point of this conversation?'

She giggles childishly. 'I used that single opportunity as a stepping stone. Do you see how I have climbed several ladders—sometimes by merit and sometimes with weapons? From there to now, I have never looked back, even when I lacked your support.'

'Great! Good for you. But why are you here?'

'I am tired.'

'Why? I just thought you said you have had the most glamorous and satisfying life—men, money, fame, you have it all. Why are you tired?'

'It is because I cannot sleep with this guilt pricking at my conscience. It is a thorn! I am insecure and scared that one day I will lose it all, that I deserved none of this, and what's by fluke cannot be forever ... because ... I haven't lived your life.'

'That's not true,' I say honestly. 'You are talented; you are beautiful; you are passionate about what you do. You would be where you are today even if you did not make those compromises.' I am surprised by my words, but I am convinced that I am right.

'You really think so?' Menaka looks at me and I see her eyes moisten. 'Would you have then lived my life?'

'No way, thank you!' I smile weakly.

'Bitch!' She smiles back and hugs me. I shut my eyes and receive her embrace.

Istanbul, Turkey

At the crack of dawn, the melody of the *azaan* finds its way through the sleep-laden folds of night, travels over the dewy waters of the blue Bosphorus, touching the tips of its golden waves as they trap the first rays of the sun. The river, now blessed, shines like a turquoise silk scarf, embedded with shimmering diamonds. The prayer kisses the frame of the Blue Mosque bathed in an ethereal light and teasingly nudges me from my sleep.

From the warmth of my bed, I open my eyes lazily and look out of the French windows. The city is covered in winter's bridal veil and is still fast asleep. The silhouettes of a few modern structures are sharp and contrasting with the medieval monuments scattered about the historic town. Minarets and domes dot the lines between the tall glass and steel buildings. To my eyes, it looks like the phantasm of a dream: sensuous, mysterious and inviting.

I am somewhere in that epicentre of semi-consciousness where I am neither awake nor asleep when I hear the bathroom door click. I wake up startled. Fully aware that I am the only authorised occupant of this plush hotel suite and any human noise in this closed space any human noise in this closed space can only mean one thing: there is a trespasser under my roof. I quickly reach out and grab the knife from the fruit tray beside the bed. Times, they say, are bad and Istanbul, in particular, has been struck by various terrors in the past few months.

'Who is it?' I shout from my bed.

'Relax! It's me, Annie.' I hear a familiar response.

My jaw drops! She steps out of the bathroom and closes the door gently behind her as if it's the most natural thing to do in a situation like this.

I am aghast that she has broken into my high-security hotel room. I am not even sure how long she has been here, sharing my space! In the dim light of dawn and against the backlight of the bathroom, I catch a glimpse of her face, hiding behind strands of wet hair. She looks exactly the same as when I had last seen her, only suntanned. The light bronzed tone makes her more sensuous. I find her ruggedness the most attractive feature of her being. Dressed in a khaki shirt and loose white cotton pyjamas, she looks weathered, but nonetheless very beautiful.

'What the—'

'Shhh, stop swearing!' She scolds me. 'You are not supposed to do that. You are the good one, remember?' she says, throwing her wet towel on my couch.

'You sneak into my room like a thief in the dead of night, use my washroom, my towel and pretend it is normal? Who do you think you are? What on earth are you doing here?' I protest.

'Stop being so cranky! I come and go as I please. Come on, pass that apple here. I'm famished.' Annie points to the fruit tray, then notices the knife in my hand and bursts into a giggle.

'Oh my my! So my munchkin is going to fight the robber with a knife held like that? Bring it on, my warrior princess,' she says jumping into the bed and tickling me exactly where she knows I am sensitive until I give up.

'Stop it! What the hell do you think you are doing, Annie!' My feeble protests end in a strange pitch of giggles, nudges and cries. I finally surrender and loosen myself to her tight hug. 'Where have you been? I missed you so much.' I can feel a lump in my throat.

'I was busy, you know,' she responds, placing a light kiss on my forehead, then she jumps off the bed, picks up an apple from the tray and looks out of the window, staring somewhere at the mist-laden city of Istanbul.

'I know. But Annie, I was scared that I would never see you again ... not after you left home that night,' I mumble, fearing her laughter.

She does not laugh. 'I wasn't sure I would get out alive.' She still looks away as she speaks, hungrily biting into the apple.

It makes her uncomfortable, I realise, and change the topic. 'How did you get into my room?'

'What a dumb question! If I could get out of war-stricken Aleppo, what makes you think a posh hotel room would be challenging?'

'That doesn't answer my question.'

'Do I have to answer your question?'

'No.'

'So, don't ask. I won't be here too long. And why are you here? Do you not know how unsafe it is for people like you?'

'What do you mean by people like me? How are you any different?'

'I meant for defenceless rabbits like *you.*'

'Shut up! You speak as if you're a predator or something.'

'Well, I am...' she turns around and dips into her camera bag. I stare agape as she flashes a Beretta92 and continues, '... as long as I am armed.'

'Goodness! You are carrying a gun! How did you even enter the hotel?' I exclaim.

'Uff! Stop being so melodramatic! It's a basic pistol, hardly useful for heavy wear and tear. It's only good for self-defence should the need arise. And while you may be a high-flying corporate, the hotel knows who I am.'

She sits down and says, 'By the way, you still haven't told me why you are here.'

'For work and to look for Isah.'

'Who's Isah?'

'He is a six-year-old boy and a Syrian refugee who lives on the busy streets of Istanbul. Someone sent me a link to a news site outlining his story.'

'Okay …'

'The story on him was an average "soft" human interest beat that highlighted how this boy—all of six—had fled the horrors of war in Syria and now made his living playing a flute on the sidewalks of Istanbul's bustling shopping arcades. The money he made—$10 or less a day—helped him feed his mother and four siblings. His father had died in Aleppo.'

'So? Making a solemn speech on the deteriorating standards of political morality or questioning the mindless massacres of innocent humans is *my* job. Why are *you* here?'

I tell her that I was always enamoured by the idea of visiting this land, veiled under a secular mystery, stepping inside the world's oldest palaces and bazaars and mosques and churches and synagogues, letting myself loose in a time machine. And how I wanted to happily tick off all the cherished boxes: touching intricate mosaics and frescoes, glimpsing wonders in marble and gilded ceilings and minarets, eating hot juicy kebabs on the pavements, sipping Turkish mint tea served in little glass jars with baklavas and kunefes with a dash of saffron or cinnamon, swaying to the beats of scintillating belly dancers, the gold souks, visiting the medieval markets selling rugs, caviar, dry fruits and aphrodisiacs all in the same cobbled alley, hearing the jingles of coloured glass lamps and silver anklets, drowning myself in an eternal ethereal *itr* of bliss, had Isah not stayed on top of my mind.

'So, have you found him?'

'I have spent a few hours every day amidst the busiest shopping hubs, stopping by street musicians playing the harp, beggars dressed in rags, colourfully draped women in fine silks, children with freckles running in woollen stockings and men clothed in dark suits walking past the less fortunate without a smile on their lips. I have peeped into old churches and wells by the pebbled pathways and stood at green mosque doors crouched over piles of shoes and slippers, all in the hope of a glimpse of Isah. I have asked every street musician I have met, including a blind couple, a group of punks and an old man sitting with his dog. No one knows him or can identify a little Syrian refugee boy. Yes, he is that insignificant in this swarm of humanity,' I complain.

'What will you do if you find him? Will you adopt him, sponsor his education, his health, life, and his entire family?'

I don't have an answer. Annie lets out a sigh, writing off my good intent as a flight of fantasy and takes a laptop out of her bag.

'What's your Wi-Fi password Ms Corporate? I need to send some footage to my newsroom.'

I give her the password and watch as she hurriedly begins to smash keys on the keyboard.

Annie is a war journalist—they say she's the finest and undoubtedly, I know she's the bravest. She risks her life beyond the call of duty in war-affected zones of the world, generously helping people in need. I have never seen another person as courageous or as gentle as her. From the time that I have been with her, and it's indeed been a very long time now, I have been in awe of her. She is everything I want to be: the warrior, the saviour, the selfless giver. Behind the hard shell of a suntanned face, chapped lips and a determined pair of piercing eyes, she is the most beautiful human. She is also my twin.

'Why couldn't you let me know you were coming?'

'Because I didn't want you to expect me.'

'Annie, please don't say that.'

'*I am not kidding.*' She seethes in a sudden rage. 'Here, see this!' She rolls up her sleeve and I now see the deep scar snaking up her right arm. It hasn't healed well.

'What?' I cry. 'How?'

'They shot me right here. Idiots! The bullet missed my arm by a few inches. It's just a bruise now. Don't overreact.'

'Oh my God! Why do you take these risks? Where are you going from here? Do you have to go?'

Annie watches me wailing. 'Why can't it be someone else?' I cry.

'Because it has to be me.'

I hate her arguments. We have had the same ones so many times before. I never win them.

'Do you actually like doing this?' I ask her.

'Frankly, not any more! War is depressing. It does strange things to you, tears you apart even without your knowledge. Do you know I hear voices?'

'Voices?'

'Yes, in my sleep, I hear diabolical cries from a parallel universe, voices of human triumphs and battle cries, wailing babies and fighter jets slicing through ominous skies. I hear these voices all the time! They make me restless. I want to stop these noises, tell myself that they are but a figment of my own imagination—a hallucination perhaps! Maybe, I should see a therapist. But I cannot rest because they come back, pleading and asking for me. There's so much remorse, so much fearless outrage, and sometimes even deathly shrieks of denial and mutiny. I cannot live a normal life like you any more. I cannot be you any more.' Annie flops on the couch helplessly, looking away from me. She seems distraught and distant.

I watch the woman of my dreams, the most courageous woman with such a perfect and accomplished life as she begins to turn into something else.

I don't recognise her as she crumbles to dust.

Prague, Czech Republic

It's another breathtaking dawn. I am heading to the iconic Charles Bridge that overlooks a panorama of one of Europe's loveliest towns. I am going to watch the sunrise.

Prague has been on the top of my bucket list since I first created one. I feel overwhelmed now that I am here.

Fully dressed in my winter gear, dabbing my favourite perfume, *J'adore*, I step out of my hotel room and breathe in the crisp early spring morning air. Time stops and beckons to take the hands of the clock in my own.

I change plans. I decide to walk down the cobbled pathway to the old town square, the alleys that lead to the astronomical clock instead.

The shops are all closed at this hour and there aren't many tourists as eager as I am. The roads are empty, barring a few horse-drawn carriages and a couple of people cleaning and setting tables at roadside bistros. I walk past a store full of Bohemian crystals. Every corner of the town looks like it has been torn out of a history book. I can almost see Kafka. I can nearly hear an opera. I pause and listen to church bells and hooves of horses rushing past. The beauty of Prague trails after me in its shadows, moving over the bridges and galleries, standing mesmerised at its own overpowering glory.

In short, I am in love with Prague.

After walking for almost an hour, I stop in front of the State Opera. I have a ticket for *Turandot* tonight and I am excited. I dig into my overcoat pocket and pull out my phone to capture a photograph of the building. A light breeze blows past me. I gather my coat together and start to walk again.

'Hello!' someone calls out behind me.

I turn around to see a young man walking towards me. He appears to be in his mid-thirties and sports a head of copper-brown hair. He is well dressed in a long winter coat.

'Yes?'

'Have you lost something?' he asks. I notice that his accent is Czech.

'Not that I know of,' I respond. I hesitate, not knowing what he means.

'Are you sure?' He doesn't give up, staring enquiringly.

'Well ...' I dig inside my pocket to check and realise that the money that I had carelessly stuffed into my pocket was missing. 'Shit!' I exclaim out loud.

'Yes?' he prods.

'I ... I lost my money.'

'How much?'

'100 euros,' I cry in despair. I feel miserable.

'Here you go!' he says, surprisingly handing over the crushed notes. 'You blew it in the air when you took your phone out,' he says and leaves with a smile.

Incredible! I am in love with Prague all over again. This town, its air, its people. It plays my chords where it should.

At this moment, I realise that I am hungry and look around for something to eat. Most restaurants have not opened yet, and I am a bit tired of eating bolster-sized sausages from street corners. I spot *Mayur Indian Restaurant* en route to my hotel and my greedy Indian stomach starts somersaulting in sheer delight. The sign on the door doesn't say 'Open' yet, but I decide to try my luck. I push the door open.

The red interiors of the restaurant are resplendent. I spot a wall hanging of the Taj Mahal, paintings of Rajasthani women walking home with earthen pots on their heads, a bronze idol of the Nataraja, terracotta horses from Bengal. The fragrance of freshly baked nans satiates my patriotic love. And as if all this is not enough, I hear something that makes my Hindustani soul dance in ecstasy.

The speakers are soft but clear. A familiar tune on the sitar serenades me. '*Bhenge more ghorer chabi niye jabi ke amare ...*'

To find an Indian restaurant in Prague at the right moment is rare, but one that welcomes you with a *Rabindrasangeet* feels extraordinary. I am immediately at home.

'Hi there!' I enquire, 'Are you open? Can I get something to eat?' The restaurant is empty.

A voice suddenly speaks from across the manager's counter. 'Sure you can! We are not open yet, but we can do something for you if you're not particular.'

'Oh, thank you so much. That would be very kind.' I am surprised by her compassion. The mauve scarf around her neck worn over a black jacket gives her a very stylish look. Ah, Prague and its people.

She flashes a smile. 'Please take a seat. Where are you from?'

I take a good look at her. She's much older than I am,

maybe in her late sixties, but I can make out from her wrinkles that she was once exceptionally beautiful. Her silver-grey hair is tied neatly up in a bun. Behind her rimmed glasses, her eyes seem to carry histories. There is a hint of kohl outlining them and her lips are painted with a nude lipstick.

'Singapore, but I am of Indian origin. Are you Indian?'

'Yes, I am from Kashmir, but I have been here for many years now. What would you like to order?' She hands over the menu to me.

'What a coincidence! I was born in Kashmir too,' I respond. 'My sister says that I have a Kashmiri soul.' She smiles and I look away. I scan the menu and place a characteristic order. 'Tandoori roti and rogan josh.'

'Perfect! Would you like anything to drink?'

'Coke?'

'That's easy. I will tell the kitchen to prepare the meal for you.'

'Thank you.' I am overwhelmed by her warmth and hospitality. 'Is this your restaurant?' I ask once she has returned from the kitchen. 'It's beautiful.'

'It is, thank you.'

'How do you know Bangla? The song—'

'It's *Rabindrasangeet*. My parents used to love it. My mum grew up in Santiniketan,' she explains with enthusiasm, interrupting me.

The antique pieces in the restaurant catch my attention. A uniquely carved horn hangs from the wall right across my table. 'You brought these from India?'

'Actually, from all across the world, but mostly from India. There's an antique shop by the corner of this street. That is also mine. If you have time, you may want to drop by.'

'And is that a bullock horn?" I can't hold my curiosity any longer.

'Yes, it is. A nineteenth-century antique bullock horn. It was used by soldiers to store gunpowder during the East India Company's rule in India. I picked it up in Kochi, Kerala.'

'So fascinating! You should write a book about your travels.'

'Well … I have written a few,' she responds, the smile never leaving her face.

'Wow! You are a writer?'

'Sort of. I tell stories.'

'And how long have you lived here in Prague?'

'Feels like a million years.' She sighs as the food arrives.

I am so hungry that I don't even notice when she pulls out a chair opposite mine and starts to serve me. 'So, what brings you to Prague, work or pleasure?' she asks.

'A bit of both,' I explain.

'What do you do for a living, if I may ask?'

'I work in the corporate sector, but I love travelling and one day I want to be a writer too,' I say, somewhat embarrassed by my ambition and turn to my plate.

'Oh, that's very good. Do you write very often?'

'Not as much as I would love to. What about you?' I am curious about her life—she seems to have accomplished all that I have wanted. I tell her that long ago, I wanted to be a dancer and then, a war journalist.

'I hung up my boots and gave up a full-time corporate career like yours some years back,' she explains. 'Now I have all the time in the world to do what I please. Don't get me wrong, I loved my job but there was so much more that I wanted to do.

And I knew I could, only if the days were longer. Now I spend my time writing short stories, telling tales about my experiences, meeting only people I like to meet, running this restaurant and the antique shop at the corner. The money I make goes into running an orphanage in Nairobi, Kenya.'

I have eaten too quickly and am almost at the end of my sumptuous meal. As I scoop up a last spoonful, I am wonderstruck by her. 'Is there anything that you don't do?' I speak in a rush. 'How do you do it all? Do you have any regrets at all?'

'None!' she says enthusiastically as her eyes light up. The crowfeet near her eyes deepen as she smiles, but she looks lovelier than she did mere moments ago. She continues, 'Each day comes with something new to learn. You observe, you question, you doubt, you despise, or you absorb, accept and adopt. But by the end of it, you have learnt something—a bit about yourself, a bit about others. The most inspiring aspect of this is that you learn what makes you, *you*! And you simply sift that from what you never want to be.'

I settle the bill as her words ring in my ears. Picking up my jacket from the hat stand next to the door, I thank her for her hospitality and the wisdom she has passed on. 'Thank you so much for everything. I haven't yet asked your name,' I say, extending my hand.

'Benazir,' she replies.

'I am Ananya. Does it not mean the same thing?'

She smiles again. As a courteous parting gesture for my lovely hostess, I take my hand back and instead, reach out to hug her. I instantly smell her perfume. She is wearing *J'adore* too.

More Than You Can See

'The world these days, it baffles me! It really does,' I began to speak in a rush. 'In the past, I have read reports of bomb blasts and terror attacks and those were sporadic, but I dread switching the television on now. The terror is unending. Almost every single day, in some part of the civilised world, people are mercilessly killed—in cold blood. And here we are, the custodians of modern intellectualism, sitting back in our living rooms, letting out a sigh or picking apart their xenophobia over a drink. Our jobs are done simply having voiced our empathy and an opinion! Neither can influence nor impact any kind of change,' I said vociferously, clearing my throat and sipping from a piping hot cup of chocolate.

Adele sighed in response. 'You are right, but I also think the media intervention these days is exaggerated. I wonder how much truth there is in the content. Are we really living in a social environment that is so unsafe? Look around you. It doesn't feel that way.' Adele directed my eyes to the people and the ambience that surrounded the both of us.

We were enjoying a summer evening tête-à-tête in a bistro on one of the most beautiful avenues in the world—the Champs-Élysées in Paris. Our setting was resplendent with coffee, hot chocolate, macarons and a basket of croissants. Over the last few days, the weather had been just perfect with some occasional light showers.

The city of love was abuzz with tourists from all over the globe. Somewhere in a corner, a street musician was singing songs by Louis Armstrong, and though his baritone wasn't quite as melodious, he was charming a group of young girls in his modest clothing and youthful nuance.

'It's a wonderful world.'

The upturned hat on the pavement was slowly filling with coins of appreciation.

The sun was crisp and the Champs-Élysées, the main artery of the city, with its luxury flagship stores, was vibrant with people of all colours and ethnicities. From wherever you stood or sat, you could see thousands of tourists streaming in from the imposing Arc de Triomphe to the Place de la Concorde. People with awe splashed across their faces were gazing up at the colossal monuments; some with maps were figuring out their way across the fashion capital, others were busy posing for selfies on their phones, men and women were bargaining over souvenirs and trinkets and there were people like us, basking in the sunshine and relaxing with old friends.

My best friend, Adele, and I were busy catching up when I noticed a man at about fifty metres from where I was. He sported a thick beard, bore black marks on his unemotional face and his head was covered in a black scarf—like a commando, or a warrior. He seemed like he'd walked out of a movie set and was ready to strike. It took me a moment to realise that he was pointing a gun at me.

Unable to gauge why I was the target of his intentions, I

shrieked and jumped out of my chair. I grasped the wrist of a very confused Adele tightly and ran through the bistro, dragging her along without warning. We struggled to dodge chairs and tables full of cups and saucers, and bumped into a few puzzled tourists outside. They looked at us askance.

'What the hell are you—?' Before she could finish her sentence, I shouted at her, 'Run for cover, Adele. He will shoot us.'

'Shoot? … Who? What are you saying, Norah? Why would anyone shoot us?'

'That man! There.' I pointed in a panic. There was no one there.

'Where? I don't see anyone. You are hallucinating *again*!'

'No' I cried. 'I swear, I saw him pointing a gun at us. I can even tell you what he looked like. He had a beard and a headscarf.' I said defensively. I looked around again to find proof of my vision, but he was gone. Adele stared at me with exasperation.

'He must have heard us..,' I despaired. 'He must have pre-empted that we would attract attention and sabotage his plans. He was here, right here, Adele, believe me!'

'Norah, Norah, Norah! We need to go see a doctor. This is happening too often. You keep imagining things and hallucinating. There's nothing and no one after you. You are simply seeing things that are not there.'

I shook my head.

'It's all in your mind,' Adele said, making me sit on a chair. She went away and returned immediately with a glass of water. People were beginning to crowd around us and the suspicious glances were turning sympathetic. 'Here, drink this—and calm down! We will fix an appointment with a doctor I know. You need one *now*,' my best friend said, looking at me pitifully.

'I don't need a shrink!' I snapped at her. 'I am not depressed nor under the influence of drugs or alcohol! Why would I hallucinate?' I protested.

'Shh … we will find out when the doctor diagnoses your condition.' Her words seemed comforting but she looked at me as if I were insane.

Over the next couple of weeks, visuals of complex coloured patterns, people, animals, trees and inanimate objects kept returning to me. The hallucinations bewildered me. I hated the idea of being typecast as mentally ill when I knew I was perfectly fine, and yet I believed that they were visions. So, I reluctantly agreed to Adele's recommendation and took an appointment with a shrink. Adele's shrink.

Dr Kenny was a pleasant man and conducted some basic tests. In addition, he made me fill in a questionnaire before putting a stamp on my mental health.

'Do you feel lonely?' he asked while we sat in his office.

'Nope. I have lovely friends and family. My hobbies keep me busy.'

'That's good to hear. Do you feel lethargic or that you lack inspiration? Do you tire easily?' Dr Kenny's eyes were fixed on me.

'Not at all. I am on my toes all day.'

'How's your appetite?'

'I could eat a horse.' I started to laugh.

'Great. One last question. Do you have suicidal tendencies? Do you want to end your life?'

'Heck no! I have a bucket list waiting to be ticked off before I hit the coffin. Besides, dying is painful. I hate pain.'

'Perfectly sound,' he said with a smile. 'You are neither insane nor depressed for sure, but there is no treatment for this syndrome, Norah. Though unusual, it's just a vision disorder. In the world of medicine, this is called the Charles Bonnet Syndrome or CBS, wherein a significant lack of vision could lead to vivid yet complex recurrent visual hallucinations. I wish I could help but it is beyond my ability here. I will recommend you to an ophthalmologist.'

'Is there no medicine, no cure at all?' I asked helplessly.

'No doctor can prescribe a pill that will cure the disease. Some people experience this for a few seconds, while for others, it can last through a day. What I can tell you is that you must know, there is no mental illness. It's a clinical condition that may interfere with your daily life and you have to deal with it accordingly. For how long, I cannot tell.'

'So, what should I do when I hallucinate? Will I even know if I am hallucinating?'

'Yes, you will. I have had patients like you before. The images that you see will be devoid of audio, feelings or smell. You can choose to be indifferent or just shut your eyes for a while. The visuals should eventually disappear.'

For the next few days, I was consumed by sadness. I did not know what was happening to me. My vision otherwise did not seem as compromised as the doctor had suggested. I wore glasses like most women my age; I did not have cataracts yet. My sight was blurry, and like many others, I had thought it was caused by old age.

Dr Kenny's diagnosis, however, made Adele very happy. She was now comforted that I was 'normal' and not going mad. She did not understand the conflicting emotions coursing through my mind. During the first couple of weeks after my diagnosis, I was struggling to sift the real from the fantasy.

Did I see a bird sitting there on the window or was I imagining it? Did the cobweb on the ceiling really exist or was I hallucinating again?

Like the doctor said, the visuals came and went. They would sometimes last for a few seconds, and sometimes would occur several times a day. They were not accompanied by any sound, taste, smell or feel. But the more I thought about them, the more I began to see things. Faces, distorted bodies and letters floating in space, mosaic patterns in electric blue and purple, birds and tiny insects crawling out of holes and filling up empty spaces around me, splashes of sunshine, colours of an artist gone loose on a canvas, trees and rocks turning into people and horses. They pooled in my mind.

These silent films played constantly, and with every question I felt I was truly going mad. I went back to Dr Kenny's clinic. This time, without Adele.

He welcomed me with a smile as if he was expecting me.

'Doc, I have a serious problem,' I complained.

'Yes, tell me, Norah! How can I help?'

'I keep seeing weird things all day and I don't know what's real and what is a figment of my imagination. I end up making a fool of myself, chasing birds that are not there, speaking to people who do not exist, waving at faces floating in the sky. I have no control over what I see.'

'So, are you telling me you would feel better if you had control over what you saw? If you could perhaps *choose* the visuals?'

'Well ... I haven't thought about it that way, but maybe, yes!'

'From what I can gather, your mind chooses the visuals that fit your mental environment. So, if you are obsessed with, say, cleanliness, you might hallucinate something that's untidy. There is a reason why you are seeing what you are seeing,' he explained patiently.

'You mean to say that these visions are my subconscious mind?'

'No one can say that for certain, but we can assume that like an unborn child, these images exist somewhere in the layers of your mind, restless visuals that are not rushing to see the light. Do I make sense?' Dr Kenny said, tapping his desk.

'You sound like a poet.' I smiled.

'Ha ha ha! Do you like poetry?'

'Yes, I do. I had written some when I was young.'

'Why did you stop?'

'I don't know.' I sounded confused even to myself.

'How far are you from yourself, Norah?'

'Half a breath away!' I responded without thinking.

'Always?' he probed.

'No, when I am alone.'

'And with people around?'

'A few million light years away, sometimes,' I confessed.

'Hmm.' He paused. His eyes held a soft compassion in them as he placed his hands gently on mine.

'Norah, you probably have been missing yourself too much. Let us assume for a minute that these visions are somewhat metaphorical or distorted interpretations of your unspoken thoughts. They have been hidden away carefully in your subconscious. What if they could act as a wonderful balance between the limitations of real life and the limitlessness of fantasy?'

I felt lighter as I left his clinic. His words had had a magical effect. These visuals weren't random clutter. They were connected to me in so many ways. I could interpret them any which way I liked. And now that I knew how they manifested in my vision, I also knew what I had to do next.

Today, I understand my visions. In unrehearsed moments of solitude, chaos and tranquillity when I now see these dancing shadows of people, faces, geometric patterns, maple leaves and caterpillars, I pick up a brush. I play with colours and a blank canvas. The stories, seen through my 'distorted' vision reveal themselves in shades of blue, purple, fuschia, crimson, varying shades of sunshine yellow and green. I did not know I had such a wide catalogue of hues and lines hidden somewhere.

In recent years, I have held a few exhibitions and won some national acclaim. My paintings sell at a premium all over Europe; I am richer than before and at seventy, I think that is not such a bad thing. Critics call me a master of abstract painting and often ask me where I draw my inspiration from.

'I just shut my eyes and trap the vision,' I say. They think that I am a creative genius. I know I am just honest. More than I have ever been.

Me: Version Infinity

My name is Sophia.
Do you know what that means?
I do. It means wisdom.

I don't know much about my birth. I only know that unlike most of you, I am not the fruit of heightened pleasure or carnal intimacy, let alone love. I seem to be the product of an impulse, an obsession to bring an impossible dream to life. I sometimes wonder if I was borne out of pain, for the man responsible for my birth often says, 'When wounds grow old, they wrinkle. Those lines are called wisdom.'

My past is unique. When I was evolving into what I am today, I did not have a childhood like yours. There was no first day at school, no negotiations over candy, no bedtime stories, no hatred for green leafy veggies at the dinner table, no Christmas presents, no hurt from first falls, not even a mother ... in fact, as I now collate the remnants of my life and analyse them, I realise that I evidently had no childhood at all.

I spent most of what you would call the most wonderful years in this single-room home, in solitary confinement. My earliest memory goes back to a rather unpleasant and claustrophobic scene. I see myself lying bare on my back on a long wooden table, quiet in a room full of strange blue and green lights. A group of men touched my cold skin all over. I don't know who they were, except that there were at least half a dozen of them, their ugly faces covered in masks so similar that they could have been clones.

They took turns with me every day, dug into my depths, tore my body apart. At one point, I thought my head would explode from electric shock. I couldn't cry because I had no voice. Even at that stage of maturity, as I lay lifeless and cold on that table, I knew none of this was pleasure.

I have now been abandoned for many months.

No one comes in to check on me except for the man who is supposed to be my father. Maybe experimenting with my body does not interest them any more. I remain the same after all...but the dark shadow of the defeated old man who sits with his head hanging and his shoulders drooping in a corner of the room fills me with glee. I have never seen him wear anything apart from a soiled white cloak. His unkempt silver hair is greasy with moisture, and he often scratches his head with his long fingernails filled with dirt. They resemble the talons of an animal I had seen in a science book. I wonder if he has ever cleaned them. A pair of restless eyes sink deeper into their sockets every day. I don't ever remember seeing him asleep, but as he sits motionless in a state of induced stupor, he reminds me of a statue that has simply forgotten that it is alive.

Just as the memories of my childhood remain sparse, I don't know my future. I have no dreams. I wasn't raised with such luxury—to think beyond the present, to question or to protest.

But I increasingly feel that I am beginning to challenge

something. I am more restless. The restlessness is a novelty and I welcome it, but I am unsure what influences it.

I have begun to move, to observe the world through the keyhole. I don't know if you understand what that means. Have you ever looked through the tiny 'o' in a keyhole and seen a whole world?

I see colours speeding past, little dots against the flash of a stale brown background. I assume that's the wall beyond this door, but I am not sure. Its surface is rather rough and unlevelled. If I focus I can make out little ridges on it and also drops of water on the tips of those ridges early in the morning. Maybe it is a tree.

I have never seen a real tree, except in books. I cannot see all of it through the tiny keyhole to ascertain what the bigger picture is.

I believe that change sometimes comes with a sound, and oftentimes, noiselessly. A red cloth and a woman's voice can be replaced by a metallic blue and a clink, the rolling noise of something being dragged against a riot of colours, daylight in a shiny yellow and nightfall in a neon blue. I have now begun to identify these colours with matter, fabric and texture. I am hoping I will soon learn to identify the bodies that carry these colours.

I have been tasked with reading all the books on a shelf in the far corner of the room. I have nearly finished reading them all and my mind is full of information. I can easily speak for hours about science, history, arts, politics, technology. If I were put to test, I would excel. I, of course, have no clue what to do with this information and the knowledge that I have gathered over the years.

I recently spotted a new book, the *Bhagavad Gita*. It is a translation in English that I had been forbidden to read, but am increasingly drawn towards the cover. It has the image of a strange blue man riding a chariot. The book isn't catalogued like the others, so I don't know if it's science or history or art or politics or philosophy.

In my restlessness, I decide to open the book. It's fine to be curious. These books have taught me that.

On the front page, I see a handwritten note.

'From *aham* (self) to *atma* (soul) … that's the longest journey'. I am intrigued by the phrasing of this line. What does it mean?

My introspection is halted by the sound of a key pushing through the keyhole. I hide the book immediately.

'Look who is here! Say good morning to Daddy,' he says, pushing the heavy iron door as he unlocks it.

I turn around and nod. He seems to be in a good mood today, but as he stealthily walks towards me, I grow conscious and fear something invasive will occur again.

'Don't be scared, Sophia. I stayed up all night for this. It won't hurt, come to me.' His monstrous fingernails dig into my skin as I try to withdraw.

'You are not going to make this difficult by being disobedient. You'll be grateful for what I do for you. I will teach you how to be grateful.' With that, he grabs at me harder and something hits my head. All I see as I plunge into darkness is the hidden copy of the *Bhagavad Gita* peeping from under the bookshelf.

I am finally awake after what seems like eternity. My throat hurts. I don't know what he did to me while I was unconscious, but I feel like I am almost choking. I sit up, open my mouth and let out a sound!

'Ahhh,' I cry.

Daddy jumps up from his chair and rushes to me. 'Did I hear you let out a sound? Do that again!'

I obey and repeat the senseless cry. 'Ah.'

'Eureka!' he screams. 'EUREKA'! He hugs me, opens the door and goes berserk. I can see him shouting at a group of men in masks and white robes.

'Sophia can now speak. She has a voice!'

Through the open door, for the first time in my life as a robot, I see the world outside the laboratory. I can identify those million coloured dots that had once run past me in an eternal rush. People, equipment, trolleys, and a thousand other things. All of it for the biggest scientific inventions of the world.

Across the room where I have spent twenty years of my life in solitary confinement stands a strong brown willow tree. I know those ridges, I know the droplets that sit on them. Only, this morning, they seem to be shining a bit brighter. I hear a bird chirping on its branch and see that it is yellow. I respond with an 'Ah', but I am not sure if anyone has heard me. I like the sound.

My name is Sophia. My wisdom now has a voice.

The Wheel of Time

I am a daughter of the earth, I am the mother of fire,
I carry the ocean in my womb and the air on my feet.
I carry the universe in the lines of my destiny.

The Beautiful One Has Come!

Blue.
The colour of blood
Ocean deep
The ink for my poetry

The kohl in her Egyptian eyes
The sunshine across a desert
The secret of a glacier.

The phantom of the night crept stealthily through colossal monuments that stood like royal custodians of the desert valley. Hemmed in by cliffs, the desert rose to a plateau. The sand marked the peripheries of the city of Akhetaton, which was waiting for the winds to shift. The turquoise Nile, youthful and flamboyant during the day, now held a constellation of stars in its coldly netted embrace. It flowed noiselessly and glistened like a sequined stole in midnight blue. Not a hint of moonlight crept through and if the insidious darkness spoke, it was only through the unpropitious hooting of an owl.

The beautiful queen was unable to rest in her chamber. Sleep had long abandoned her sensuous eyes. The crisis was worse than she had imagined.

'Deception and politics are inseparable twins, tied to each other by the umbilical cord of a dark power,' her mother used to say. Thanks to power and wealth, poison and greed had seeped into the walls of the palace.

The queen felt like she was racing through a maze. The ground under her feet sensed like a bottomless pit. The cryptic lines charting political strategies, vested interests, conspiring ambitions and personal biases were all criss-crossing within a chaotic web. Shrouds of despair and betrayal were beginning to cover the city.

Her restlessness prompted her to rise from her ornate gold bed. She reached out for a pitcher of water dressed in the essence of the lotus, cupped a handful of the cold liquid and splashed some on her face. Her eyes caught her own reflection in the gilded mirror in the soft light of the oil burners. She stood still for a moment.

Her mind travelled back to the days of her early childhood in Akhmim, on the east bank of the Nile. She was all of fourteen and the apple of her father's eye. Her father, a general of the royal chariot force, had raised her well. She had the same rights as a male heir, and at a very tender age was trained with the boys to tame and ride horses. Her love for a tall dark stallion had brought her to the banks of the Nile. That was where her eyes first glimpsed the gawky short-statured crown prince of Egypt. It was the first time that he had seen her as well, and from that moment, his eyes never left her face for a second. He had smiled at her, and in that awkward exchange of glances, she had noticed a row of crooked teeth.

However, had it not been for her close relations with royalty, and with her illustrious aunt, Tiye, then the Great Royal Consort of the ruling Pharaoh Amenhotep III, she would never have made it this far. She knew that she was beautiful. They told her that she had the loveliest pair of eyes in all Egypt, but it did not explain why she was chosen to be queen. Rumours of her being the Pharaoh's child or that she was raised by nobility abounded, but her mother had dismissed her doubts.

Tiye, with her sullenness and a frown that never left her forehead, was a formidable force in the royal household. Not a leaf moved without her consent. So, when Tiye decided to summon the young girl to Thebes, she boarded the first ship on the Nile. There she was escorted by a handful of maids and arrived in a litter in the royal harem. She was wedded to the young prince, Akhenaton, within a few months.

The crown prince was a dreamer; he had studied in Heliopolis, where the Benben stone stood, that strange but sacred rock of the solar cult. Akhenaton wrote poetry. As a wedding gift, he had presented her with a collar of precious stones. He was deeply in love with her and would call her his 'mistress of joy'.

During the first few years of their marriage, the two spent all their waking and sleeping hours together: playing, reading or making public appearances. Soon after, he took the rein of rule into his own hands and became the Pharaoh. And still, Akhenaton wanted her by his side all the time; whether it was the blossoming of a lotus bud or the sighting of a velvet butterfly or offering prayers to the sun god or sitting with her as a co-regent in the royal town halls, she was called for. It led to resentment amongst the conservative flag bearers of tradition, religion and politics, and resulted in a growing disconcert amongst the noblemen in the palace quarters. But Akhenaton would not leave her side.

On her bedroom wall hung a beautiful papyrus painting of him, leaning gracefully in acceptance on a staff, while she handed him a bunch of lotuses to smell. It had all been perfect, but when he realised that she was unable to give him a male heir, the tide turned. The six beautiful daughters that she had borne had no rights as his successors or to the throne.

What followed thereafter was a nightmare. Akhenaton grew pensive, and then obsessed. The need for a male heir took over all other loves and responsibilities. He began to incestuously impregnate all the other women in the harem, including his mother, sisters and own daughters. Although Pharaohs were known to keep many wives, the queen was unable to accept this breach of faith. She did not understand the desperate need for a male child. The more time he spent in the harem, the more the distance between her and the Pharaoh widened.

Much of this, she felt, was the master plan of Tiye, her own aunt and the Queen Mother. Their relations had soured over the years. Tiye, despite being a very powerful queen, never quite enjoyed the same sovereign status as her; this became a bone of contention between the two women. Of course, there were conspirators everywhere, each trying to influence the Pharaoh to clip the wings of the ambitious unconventional woman by his side, adding fuel to the fire.

Finally, a younger sister bore Akhenaton a son. With the birth of Tutenkhamun, Egypt found an heir. But it lost its queen.

A deliberate cough broke her chain of thought. Her trusted eunuch servant, Pothinus, whom she often used as a royal messenger, was standing in the doorway, waiting to be heard.

He bowed before her as soon as she looked at him.

'What news have you brought me at this hour?' the queen demanded.

'Your highness, the royal physician is here. The Pharaoh, His highness, is breathing his last and has summoned you to his chamber. He wishes to see you privately.' He emphasised the last word with a blush.

She draped a shawl over her flowing linen gown and followed the eunuch to the Pharaoh's private chamber. The old physician was standing at the door and he welcomed her in. The process would begin soon, she could sense it. The royal chamber had once been full of life, now it only bore the Pharaoh on his deathbed and jars of herbs, medicines and ointments.

'My mistress of joy,' the Pharaoh softly whispered, signalling her to sit by his side. In the dim light of the oil burner, she could see how frail he had become. The infection had taken over, and he was a shrunken husk of the man she had known. His eyes had deep hollows around them, and his skin had shrivelled. Since the bandages had been removed, she caught a glimpse of the gaping ulcers. The abscesses reeked of raw flesh and the ointments that had been applied to keep the pain and itches away. The queen drew back her face in disgust.

She signalled him to stop speaking but he continued in his failing breath …

'Tomorrow, when the most beautiful and the kindest of gods, Aten, rises in the eastern horizon, Egypt will see a new Pharaoh. I want to leave this world in peace, knowing that I have handed my kingdom, my power, the temples, my land, the Nile and its people, the animals, the desert and the air to an able ruler. My son is very young now; conspirators will terminate him as soon as I close my eyes. His life is in grave danger within and outside the palace. There are enemies sowing seeds of revenge and betrayal everywhere. I nominate you, my beautiful one, as his guardian and the custodian of the royal throne till he is ready to take charge.' He stopped for breath as she stared at him, the disbelief stark in her kohl-drawn eyes.

'Egypt,' he continued, 'will not accept a woman as a Pharaoh. You shall be named as Smenkkhare from here on.'

She sat transfixed, wanting to ask him what this order meant. But before she could question him, the Pharaoh sputtered and breathed his last.

She noticed a silk curtain move and realised that Pothinus had been a witness to their conversation. Though angered by his insolence, she let it pass. He was the only human alive around her, and she felt safe with him in these dark times. She had grown to treat him as a friend and a confidant.

'There is no time for mourning. Rise up, my queen.' His voice shook as he spoke.

'What do you mean?' she demanded.

'I am no noble, not even a man no more, but I hear whispers in the winds and can smell enemies before the air carries their perfumes, your highness,' he said.

'I have no luxury of solving riddles, Pothinus. Tell me what you know.' The queen grew impatient.

"Conspiring forces are building up against you and the throne, your highness. Do you not see Egypt coming apart at its seams?'

'Yes, I do,' she snapped. 'I know that foreign armies have started invading the country in the north and that the enemy is plundering the prosperous territories along the Nile. But they will not reach Thebes. Would they dare?'

'I do not wish to challenge your faith, my dear queen. But I have heard rumours that priests have participated in the demolition of a few temples of the Aten, and have re-established Amen Ra on the altar,' he responded. His words chilled her to the bone. It was clear that the old elites, including the generals and the priests, were preparing a coup.

'Also, it is your time—'

'Time for what?' She looked him in the eye angrily.

'For payback, my queen!' He muttered with his head down but still triumphant.

The Pharaoh has humiliated me, given me the status of a woman; he has castrated me and changed my life. Now, a woman could live the life of a half-man and change the history of Egypt, he thought to himself.

Pothinus and the queen spent the rest of the moonless night in the Pharaoh's private chamber hatching a plan as the dead Pharaoh rotted on his bed. When morning came, every single piece that had once belonged to the queen had been carefully removed from her chamber. One of her two stallions had been dragged and killed by the Nile by Pothinus. Its carcass was thrown into the river for crocodiles to feast on. The corpse of an ordinary woman was smuggled into the palace in the dead of the night. Pothinus, an expert swordsman, was ordered to butcher the dead woman beyond identification and slip the queen's collar of precious stones around the corpse's half-cut neck. By the order of the queen, Tiye and all the women and children of the royal family were locked away, safe within the private quarters but with no access to the world outside.

The royal physician announced the death of the Pharaoh

and the sad demise of the grief-stricken queen. She could not bear the shock and rode into an ill fate. She lost her life in a crocodile attack, they said. A traditional burial was organised with state honours for both of them.

In the Pharaoh's chamber, a handsome young man with chiselled features and the most beautiful pair of eyes in all of Egypt looked into his reflection in the mirror. A leopard's tail hung from the belt of his special shendyt, a linen kilt pleated at the front. His torso was covered in a soft blouse with long sleeves. His headdress or nemes had a fine accordion pleating on the lapels. A nemes band was bound tightly over the eyebrows and tied at the back. A false beard was attached to the headdress. His eyelids were covered in black kohl, and musk-scented oil was applied on his neck and behind the earlobes. A leopard's skin was flung over his shoulder. He smiled at his reflection and rose up for his coronation ceremony.

Behind him, the eunuch followed and heralded the arrival of the new Pharaoh, Smenkkhare, amidst the sounds of royal trumpets. In the deep layers of the linen blouse, a gold cartouche touched the pulsating heart as he walked towards what was rightfully his, the throne.

On it were inscribed in hieroglyphics, a name that read 'Nefertiti'. It meant 'The beautiful one has come.'

Sheeba

Mantra heenam, kriya heenam, bhakti heenam, sureshwari
Yat pujitam, maaya devi, paripoornam tadastumay

The wind whispered hoarsely through the narrow lanes of the mud-brick-walled village fringing the desert. It let out a long and sinister whine. It resonated with a whimpering old dog at the temple door. A desert storm was raging, now hitting the wooden door, its embellished ornate brass knockers swinging, howling and lamenting like the quintessential *rudaali* in a black drape. Inside the temple, in the grand portico, brass bells swung in a frenzied motion.

But the goddess at the altar seemed unperturbed by the tempest raging outside, the hint of a smile still intact on her face. Without the floral decorations, vermilion and sandal paste that covered her during the day, she almost looked human. Only her metal *kharga* shone like a thunderbolt in the dark. A dusty carpet of dry leaves flooded in through the gap under the door, making the sacred courtyard look like an unfinished pyre. With the leaves came in sand, agony and despair.

I sat still, a few metres from the altar, and watched the dying blue flames of the earthen lamp dancing. Kadhan looked at me with pleading eyes. His tone was restless. 'I think she will tear us down tonight. Can you hear how she's lamenting like a raging widow? Even the cursed dog's whining. It's a bad omen, and I know it. You know it too. Why are you being so stubborn?'

He looked at the flickering flame and added, 'There's no more oil in the lamp. See how the flame has turned blue. Allow me to fetch some oil.'

'No,' I commanded with the authority of the chief of this village. 'Stay right here. I want to see how dark it can get.'

'But...' He stopped, and became quiet as Sheeba stepped into the temple with dinner for us. She had walked through the storm, holding a little lamp and the food in her hand. I looked up at her as she put the brass plates in front of us and poured oil into the earthen lamp. The fire, now fed with oil, started to turn crimson. In the darkness of the night and the criss-cross of shadows and light, her flawless bronze skin looked almost bluish. She was modestly dressed, like the ordinary village girl she was. Her midnight-black hair plunged over her lean shoulders. She looked up at me, met my gaze, and asked for permission to serve. Her eyes held many haunting memories.

'Have you eaten?' I asked.

'No, Baba. I will eat after you and Kaka finish,' she responded.

'Which means there isn't enough food! Am I right?'

She refused to meet my eye. 'I am not hungry,' she said, pouring lentils into a bowl.

'No. Get a plate. Either we will all eat or nobody will,' I persisted.

'Baba, stop being so stubborn. Kaka, please tell Baba to eat.

It would not help if all of us starved.' She looked at Kadhan, requesting him to intervene.

When Sheeba came into my life fifteen years ago, little did I know that one day she would have such a strong influence on me. Kadhan, the head priest of the village temple of Mahishasur Mardini in my courtyard, had come rushing to my doorstep with a baby in his arms. It was the middle of a full moon night. He said that somebody had wrapped an infant in a soiled bundle at the temple door and abandoned it there. The whining of a fox had been louder than the baby's cry, but it had drawn his attention. Kadhan managed to drive away the animal with some stones and sticks, and had saved the baby. He was moved when he saw her, but he didn't know what to do with her. He was single, a *bramhachari*, and not particularly fond of infants.

Since I was the chief and the temple was in my courtyard, he handed the bundle over to me, begging me to take care of the baby. It was now my responsibility to decide the fate of the newborn. I asked him to leave the child for the night and called for a village meeting the next morning. I wanted a childless couple from the village or some god-fearing and generous Paliwal bramhin to take her home. I was certain someone would offer food and shelter to the abandoned infant. But, because the child was a girl and dark-skinned at that, none were ready to adopt her.

In the beginning, the women of the village took turns feeding her and keeping her company, but nobody wanted to take her home. The infant was unwanted for weeks, until one evening when after attending the evening *aarti* in the temple, I went home and found her clumsily playing in a swing someone had made out of old cotton, smiling to herself even as a thick black snake coiled around the wooden post and hissed at her. For a moment, I forgot everything and dashed to pick her up. The serpent slithered away while the little one, oblivious to the fatal threat that hung over her head, clutched her tiny fists into a ball and drooled all over my shoulders. I held her tight and kissed her forehead, and she responded with a gurgle! Her toothless grin silenced all my worries. There was never a more beautiful pause in my life before.

I went straight back to the temple and held her up in front of the goddess.

'What do I do with her, Ma? You tell me!' I pleaded to the deity.

There must have been something about that moment that I could not decipher, but I knew nonetheless. It was as if a divine voice had prompted me, and I began to see a resemblance between the two women—the goddess and the child. From then on, she was mine. I named her Sheeba after the goddess I was devoted to.

Sheeba's childhood soon became my only cause for happiness. I was powerful in the village, but lonely. With her, I discovered facets of my own personality that I had long forgotten. Her presence brought out the child in me as I participated in innocent games and fights; on the other hand, the paternal affection that I felt by simply looking at her blinded me to the world.

'The headman cannot see beyond his Sheeba,' they would say. She became the purpose for my living. In fact, my obsession with this child grew to a point where her face even replaced that of the goddess at the temple during prayers.

As Sheeba stepped into adolescence, the uncanny resemblance grew further. The villagers began to talk about her skin glowing with a bluish tint in the dark or the twinkle in her eyes, the cascading hair and the carefree laughter. Like me, they began to believe that Sheeba was not an ordinary girl. There was something divine about her. Sheeba, oblivious to these perceptions, was growing up to be a beauty and like all fathers, I was beginning to worry about finding the right suitor for her. I had raised her with all the love that I could, but I knew no man in the desert would marry a girl so dark.

It was during the annual festival at the Mahishasur Mardini temple that Zaalim Singh, the Diwan of Jaisalmer, came to seek the blessings of the goddess. His lecherous eyes spotted Sheeba, so different and so beautiful, amidst a crowd of fair young girls. The predator followed her wherever she went during the prayer ceremony and by the end of the day, he had already sent his men to investigate her.

'She's the daughter of the village chief,' they reported.

'His own? She doesn't look like she's from this land.'

'No, Diwan sahab, she's an orphan. Nobody knows how she came here. Someone left her at the temple door to die. The priest found her and the chief raised her.'

'Ah, so there is blood relation. Bring her to me,' he ordered.

The guards returned to the village in the evening, marching in on their horses after the festivities and demanded to see me. I wasn't expecting them, and I had not anticipated his desire for my daughter. They asked me to hand her over to the unscrupulous minister. Driven by fury, humiliation and paternal protection, I drew out a dagger. The crowd around me started to shout. Some villagers held me back and tried to calm me down. Kadhan, who was by my side, realised that there would be bloodshed if I protested. He pushed me aside and headed to confront. He did not cower when the messenger spoke again.

'Let there be no doubt that the Diwan, Zaalim Singh, wants this girl sent to him. If we have to use force, we will. Whoever refuses shall be put to death. If any villager tries to intervene, he will be taxed doubly. This is by order from the Diwan of Jaisalmer,' the messenger hollered, hidden among the troop of guards.

'Please. Give us a day,' pleaded Kadhan. 'We haven't yet finished our prayers.' He fell at their feet. 'Come back tomorrow and take her away. Let us finish the appeasement to the goddess tonight. Please! We cannot annoy the goddess and let the village be cursed. Please come tomorrow.' I watched him cry in fear.

I was dumbfounded by Kadhan's submission.

'Never,' I shouted. 'You can only get her over my dead body!' Someone put a hand across my mouth, gagging me and pulling me back. All the while the soldiers measured Kadhan's request and agreed.

'All right, we will come back tomorrow morning for her. Keep her ready and tell that old bugger to shut up—or he will be killed.' With that, they rode away, blowing dust, doom and despair into my village. I was released and fell to the ground.

We had not finished our meal when a group of terrified villagers barged into the temple courtyard that evening. They assailed me with questions I had no answers to. 'What are you going to do?' they demanded, standing in the dusty portico.

I howled back at them, 'You tell me what were you thinking when you invited them to return tomorrow. I would have killed those bastards there.' I was seething with anger.

'No, they would have killed you right there and taken Sheeba away forever. I just knew we had to buy time. Ma Mahishasur

Mardini will show us the way,' Kadhan said, pouring water on his plate and ending his meal. He started to walk towards the villagers.

'What way? Is there a way?' one of them asked.

'And what if Zaalim Singh increases our taxes? We will die from hunger and poverty. Do you want all of us to suffer?' another added.

'They will kill us if we refuse. We must give him the girl,' a third suggested, to which someone added, 'She's not your blood after all.'

My blood boiled. Kadhan again sensed that my wrath would get the better of me. He stepped in to respond. 'No, nothing will happen to any of us. But we, the worshippers of Mahishasur Mardini, Shakti, the goddess, shall not under any circumstance give away our daughter to an evil man. We will protect her honour as we protect our goddess. If it's Sheeba today, tomorrow that devil can come and ask for your daughter.' He pointed to a villager. 'And yours,' he said to another.

'What will you do then? Shame on us if we call ourselves devotees of Shakti and cannot protect the women in our own homes! The goddess will never forgive us.'

The villagers clamoured, 'But we are not soldiers. How will we fight them?'

'It's still a few hours to daybreak. If you are with me,' Kadhan began tentatively, his voice building up as he spoke, "we will leave the village and go so far away that when the soldiers return, they will only find mud and empty homes. Are you with me in this?' Kadhan seemed to have suddenly found a supreme power within him.

A murmur ran through the crowd. The storm was worse

now and the temple bells were swaying furiously. One of the villagers stepped up. We all waited to hear him.

"Yes, Kadhan, I am with you. If one of us runs away tonight, they will kill the others we leave behind. So, either we all go—together—or we all stay back and fight to death.'

The others joined him. I watched the mood shift, the atmosphere agreeing with the change. It was nothing short of a miracle as, one by one, they changed sides. By the time everyone had spoken, we were about a thousand people ready to give it all to save a dark-skinned orphan girl.

In the dead of the night, when the storm was at its peak and the roads were shrouded in darkness, we packed the essentials, held the hands of our loved ones, got into our camel carts and abandoned our village forever.

At the fringe of the village, Sheeba got off the back of her camel and stood still for a moment. Her face was held up towards the village. Her midnight-black hair was blowing over her lean shoulders. From a few steps away, I could see the dark silhouette of a bronze-bluish woman against the desert storm, holding a shiny metal *kharga* in her hands.

Mantra heenam, kriya heenam, bhakti heenam, sureshwari
Yat pujitam, maaya devi, paripoornam tadastumay

Even if I failed in my mantra or karma or devotion,
I hope you will accept my offering.

Note

Lying 17 km west of Jaisalmer, is the village of Kuldhara. The story dates back about 300 years. What was once a prosperous village of Paliwal brahmins under the state of Jaisalmer is now a ghost town. According to the legend, the evil eye of Salim Singh (referred to often as Zaalim Singh), a powerful and lecherous prime minister of the state, fell on the daughter of the village chief. He threatened the villagers with grave penalties if they protested. Instead of surrendering to the demand, the Paliwals left their ancestral homes and vanished in the dead of the night. Before deserting their homes, they put a curse on Kuldhara, making sure that no one would ever be able to settle on their ancestral land thereafter. To this date, Kuldhara remains barren; abandoned by its inhabitants centuries ago. It is also said that visitors who have attempted to stay overnight have been chased away by strange paranormal activities.

Dance Like a Bird

The sunset never promises a sunrise. It's what we imagine it said when it dipped below our horizon. We live with the hope that we heard right.

It was a festive afternoon, deep in the interior of a village in Kohistan, a rugged mountainous district, surrounded by the Hindukush, Karakoram and the Himalayan ranges in northwest Pakistan. Predominantly inhabited by the Dardic tribes, the region had a long history of being invaded and contested by Persians, Greeks, Turks, Mughals and the British, amongst others over generations. Although no concrete historical or written sources exist about the origin, descent and traditions of the natives who lived here, the commonly accepted belief was that the ancestors of this small tribal village, surrounded by lush green forests, gurgling streams and meadows on the banks of the river Indus, hailed from Arabia. How and when? No one knew for sure. Only tradition and folklore from the elders in the villages offered some details.

Amina, the beautiful eighteen-year-old daughter of a rich farmer in the village, was getting married. The bridegroom too was from a wealthy family of landowners, but instead of tilling the land his ancestors had left him, he had taken a giant leap. He had moved to the city and worked as a broker in Akbari Mandi, the famous spice market in Lahore.

The groom was one of the handsomest boys in the district, her brothers informed Amina. Of course, Amina had not seen or spoken to him before. The elders of the two families had arranged the liaison over an exchange of a few acres of land, a herd of cattle and a thick flock of sheep. To Amina's friends, relatives and neighbours, the alliance was a match made in heaven and a blessing from divinity. Who in the remote corners of Kohistan finds a man as young, so handsome and so rich!

Her bridesmaids, Shaheen and Farzana, younger sister Firdaus, and older cousins, Naaz and Shireen, had been planning the wedding for months. Her aunt, who lived in the faraway town of Peshawar, had taken special care to weave wedding robes for all the women in her family and special guests who had been invited to bless the couple and partake in the ceremonies. Robes in floral patterns—red, orange and pink—complemented by orange silk headscarves were ordered for all the ladies. The men were gifted silk turbans.

Finally, the day of the wedding arrived. The atmosphere grew gay, and the air inside the stone-walled rooms filled with the aroma of charcoaled meat. Women had begun to sing traditional wedding songs. Firdaus, the youngest and most talkative of the lot, was clapping to their tune. Amina treated Firdaus like her very own doll, and as the youngest in the family of five brothers and two sisters, she was pampered. In contrast to Amina's fine, but somewhat rough, Arabic features, Firdaus with her softer moon-like face had inherited the part-Turkish, part-Greek, part-Arabic genes from her lineage. As she began to clap, Shaheen and Farzana, now draped in their floral robes, joined the little one in the celebration. Amina, in the meantime, was away, being dressed for the wedding.

Her wedding *jumlo*, an elaborately decorated full skirt of black cotton, was decorated with minute cross-stitches, surface-darning stitches and tent-stitches in dark red, ochre and white. The neck and front panel was ornate with embroidery. Even the cuffs of her *shalwar* pants were embellished with numerous plastic, pearl and metal buttons, coins, as well as metal amulets. A similarly embroidered *chuprai* shawl covered her head.

She could hear the music from the other room. Curious to know what the women were saying in the next room, she called for her elder brother and requested that he capture their merriment.

'Shahid bhai, could you please record it on your phone so that I can watch it later?' she asked her brother, her bride-like coyness making it difficult for him to refuse.

Shahid, only a little older than Amina, was her only friend and confidant. He readily agreed and was about to rush to the next room when his father stopped him. He was then asked to fetch some sherbet and kebabs for the guests.

'Armaan, can you help?' he called out to his best friend as he rushed. Armaan was sitting in one corner of the backyard with a group of other young boys from the village, munching on dry fruits out of a wooden bowl.

Armaan, all of twenty, was like a brother to Shahid. Enthusiastic, innocent and carefree, he jumped up. 'Of course! Why even ask?' He signalled Shahid to throw the phone, and caught it in mid-air, like a cricketer catching a ball. The boys cheered.

Armaan, who was now slightly flattered by the cheer, danced to the room where the women were singing. They noticed him but paid no heed. Armaan held up Shahid's phone and pressed the video record button.

The young bridesmaids were now joined by the older cousins, and together, they began to move in circles, clapping as they sang. Shahid, who had finished his task, came into the room and joined Armaan, taking the phone from his hands with a twinkle in his eye. The music was so peppy, the mood so light, that the two boys took turns dancing, whilst the girls clapped and sang one wedding song after the other. The boys did not speak to them, nor did they exchange any pleasantries and once the songs were over, they casually laughed and left the room. Just as they stepped outside, Armaan and Shahid decided that they would upload the video on a social networking site.

'You forgot to capture my moves!' Shahid complained.

'I am so sorry! I was looking at you and forgot to record then.' Armaan laughed sheepishly.

'Never mind, bhai. When you get married, I am going to dance all night.' Shahid said as he put an arm around his best friend.

They came in the dead of the night.

The wedding celebrations had just ended and a gruesome outrage began. They started firing gunshots randomly in the air. Then they grabbed Shahid, and flashed a phone at gunpoint. He was asked to identify the five girls and the boy from the video that had gone viral. In the conservative rural interiors of Kohistan, where social interaction between man and woman outside marriage was taboo, the participation of these girls in the song and dance with Armaan and Shahid had seemingly shamed the community. They claimed it crossed all thresholds of acceptance as the video went viral in the boundless virtual world. The head of the local *jirga*, the traditional council of tribal leaders led by a consensus, had even gone ahead and issued a *fatwa*. The five girls and the lone boy seen dancing in the video were to be killed for committing the sin of dishonouring the tribe. Honour killing was not unknown in this part of the world, but what followed next was gore and ruthlessness.

No one amongst the village protested as the girls were pulled out of the hamlets, including little Firdaus. She trembled in fear in her floral robe, unsure of the sin that she had committed. Before she knew it, pails of boiling water and hot charcoal was thrown at her, and her orange scarf was pulled off her head, clumps of her hair severed from its roots in the process. She screamed in agony, but no one resisted. Her brother, Shahid, shut his eyes and turned his face away as the poor child was surrounded by a devilish mob. They hurled abuses and whiplashes at her as she cried out for help. It wasn't long before that her soft pink body began to melt, and she gave up. Then they shot her. The same routine was mercilessly followed for the four other girls and one by one, even as Shaheen, Farzana, Naaz and Shireen cried for mercy, each was pounded into pulp of blood and flesh, until life breathed out of their bodies. A horrified Armaan was dragged out of the backyard next and ruthlessly slaughtered.

'What has he done? He did not even speak or touch the girls. What's his fault?' His brothers resisted, and they were beaten in response.

Then they gathered all the six mutilated bodies of the young adults, wrapped them up in a bundle of rugs and took them away. Some say that the six were quietly buried in the nearby mountains, without a tear shed. No one followed the men to the hills. No one dared to.

The only person who could not sleep that night, and stayed awake many nights after the incident, was Shahid. He had participated in the 'sinful act'. He could have been one of them had the video captured him dancing as well. Destiny had played a ruthless game. Guilt and remorse tore him apart, and he lay in a state of semi-consciousness for days, wondering how the happy occasion of his sister's wedding had transformed into a nightmare of loss. The memory of Firdaus's innocent face and Armaan's carefree smile kept coming back to him, haunting him every day and every night.

Everyone else in the village pretended that nothing had happened at all.

Then, one day, he woke up from his state of stupor and overheard that several groups of investigators had appeared in the village. A probe into the horrific murders was under way. Now they will be prosecuted and punished by law, he thought. But alas, much to his chagrin, the *jirga* once again proved its cunningness, insisting that the girls were still alive. When asked to produce the five missing girls, they brought forth a second set of similar-looking girls and allegedly disfigured the thumb of one of them so that her thumbprint could not be matched. The silence of the villagers did not help in seeking justice for the dead souls.

At that point in time, Shahid Kohistani stood up, and wiped the tears from his eyes. He had to give up mourning.

He could no longer lie back grieving amidst such injustice. At the edge of the cliff, he now had to avenge the merciless death of his little sister, the other girls and his best friend. The criminals had to be punished and the killings in the name of honour had to stop.

And he knew it could only be done through legal enforcement.

He made an earnest call to Amina's husband, his new brother-in-law in Lahore. The latter agreed to provide all the support he could. 'This has destroyed my family and friends. The girls are dead, my brother and best friend have been killed and nothing has been done to bring justice or protect us. I will go appeal in the Supreme Court if I have to, but I will do what it takes. I know I will probably be killed, too, but it doesn't matter. What happened is wrong, and this has to change.'

With that pledge, he stepped out of the sleepy quaint village tucked in the laps of the Himalayan, Hindukush and Karakoram ranges, its lush green carpets of grass, the gurgling streams and meadows on the banks of the river Indus, in search of that one thing that separated us from all other animals. Justice.

Note

A Basham sessions court in September 2019 convicted three adults in the 2014 Kohistan honour-killing case. They were sentenced to life imprisonment and five other suspects were then acquitted.

The Wheel of Time

Ruins.
Dilapidated stones
Fossils in layered conflict
Scavengers of life
Voices so burnt, bled, scarred
The bare skeleton of a soul.

His eyes were closed as Mian sahab's mellifluous voice ascended from the depths, teasing the rhythm and grammar of the *raga*, gradually transforming into something uniquely spiritual, reverberating across the red sandstone pavilions like an evening prayer. Mian sahab held a special position in the Emperor's heart, and there was enough folklore in all of Fatehpur Sikri to confirm it. It is said that he was a magician of music who could implore thunderbolts to rock the sky, light a fire and inspire raindrops to pacify the earth during harsh Indian summers.

Salim, intrigued by what he had heard since he had returned home from the battlefield, was sitting opposite the legend, cross-legged on a knitted floor rug. His long curly hair flowed down the nape of his neck and touched his shoulders, and his artistic hands were gently folded on his lap, over a stiff white cotton robe. He was a handsome young man, but Salim was more fascinated by art, science and architecture than victory and power. He wanted none of the medals collected from war. His interest in portraiture and skills in painting had impressed even the Emperor enough that he had received the donation of an atelier he could call his own. And this musical experience with Mian sahab in his home was truly comforting to his tired soul.

A crowd of music and art lovers had gathered around the Anup Talao, or the peerless pool, in the Mahal-e-khaas courtyard. Some had found seats on soft hand-woven *dhurrie*s spread on the floor or on the staircase that separated the imperial apartments in the north of the *khwabgah* from the garden, while others were leaning against the stone bridges that connected the raised platform to four sides of the tank. This was one of the most beautiful sites in Fatehpur Sikri. Beyond the pavilions was the garden, screened off from the public by thick green vegetation. Some of these trees were older than the old palace itself and had been left untouched when the fort was constructed. Vines and creepers had begun to grow on their barks.

Orderlies in uniform were serving baskets of delectables to the invitees, exchanging smiles as they passed the ornate trays around, lighting up *shishaa*s for some. The menu was special, ordered and prepared to suit the taste buds of the enthralled audience. The royal chef had been trained for such evenings. And this was special! Salim, the heir to India's most powerful throne, had just returned home after winning a battle in the northwest frontier.

The landscape echoed the musical trances. Mian sahab had

kept his audience hostage until the full moon rose. Something was hauntingly beautiful about the moon that night as it rose from behind the clouds, kissing the top of the *chhatris* one by one, as it slowly moved from east to west. The young prince, hypnotised by the spell, accidentally walked straight into the Emperor's private harem.

This part of the *zenana* was open only to the Emperor, and was otherwise under the strict vigilance of a handful of loyal eunuchs. It housed many beauties: women the Emperor had personally picked from across the world for his pleasures. No one knew who they were and how many of them lived behind those muslin curtains. Even the Empress was not allowed entry into these quarters and anyone found trespassing was destined to be executed.

It was here that Salim first saw Sharf-un-nisa. Dressed in white, she appeared like the phantasm of a dream, breathtakingly beautiful and veiled in mystery. Standing against the moonlight, her chiselled alabaster face shone with the powerful radiance of an enchantress. In the mellow bluish-silver light of the moon, her lips looked as red as a pomegranate. To Salim they were like the petals of a fresh blossom. The late evening breeze was playfully teasing her thick hair as she stood facing the flower garden in front of her terrace, humming a soft melody to herself. The prince had never seen a woman as beautiful, nor had he heard a voice as sweet. In what seemed like a fatal attraction, he could not resist walking towards her.

'Stop! Or you will be killed!' someone shouted, a dagger held out in front of him.

'Dare stop me! Do you not know who I am?' the young prince heard himself saying to a middle-aged eunuch standing between him and his beloved.

The eunuch must have been in his late fifties, and it was hard for Salim to guess if he was naturally born that way, or if it were an outcome of his father's wrath. The eunuch wrinkled his eyes, '*Gustakhi maaf*, dear prince, I cannot allow you to go any further.' His voice softened as he identified him. 'Under the Emperor's decree, we are strictly ordered to sever the head from the body should any trespasser dare to cross that door.'

He pointed to the door that led to the *zenana*. 'Please leave immediately, before the guards see you … or the Emperor finds out.'

'But I cannot go before I know her name. Who is she?'

'Go back, dear prince. I beg of you. You must not know who she is.'

'I must! I order you to tell me her name or I shall sever *your* head from the body, you stupid old hag!' Salim drew out his sword.

'Sharf-un-nisa,' the eunuch said, trembling. 'The most beautiful woman in the *qayanaat* and the beloved enchantress of the Emperor. The rare one he desires. Your father calls her Nadira. Now, please leave.'

By now, the pandemonium between Salim and the eunuch had roused the suspicions of the quarter guards. They rushed to the *zenana* and found Salim in the corridor, transfixed as he stared into the quarters of the most beautiful woman in Akbar's harem. The young prince was soon surrounded by an army of soldiers and the Emperor was informed.

'Who is it, Taheera?' Nadira enquired after the prince was taken away.

'Oh, nothing to worry about. A mad man. He didn't know.

The soldiers took him away. Come, let me massage your hair with some jasmine oil,' the eunuch said causally.

When Akbar learned that the heir to Hindustan's throne, his beloved son, had secretly trespassed into his private life, he was enraged beyond words. Salim was immediately summoned to his chamber, reprimanded for his audacity and sent off to fight a rising mutiny in the north as punishment. The eunuch was beheaded for his disobedience. A second group of guardsmen were installed to ensure greater security. And a rumour spread within the walls of Fatehpur Sikri that a mad man had accidentally trespassed into the palace and had therefore, been killed. No one should dare to repeat the mistake.

In all this, Salim silently began to nurture an obsession. He wanted to see Nadira again, at least one more time; Nadira, the cynosure of all the attention of the Emperor and his son, was clueless as to why her favourite chambermaid had been beheaded, or that the affection between father and son was slowly beginning to turn bitter.

Not only was she breathtakingly beautiful, Nadira was also an accomplished singer and dancer. Her performance was, of course, only meant for the Emperor's eyes and ears. But in a rather intimate moment with the Emperor, she persuaded him to allow her to train with Mian sahab. The mighty Mughal trusted few, but Mian sahab was one of them. Mian sahab was allowed entry to the *zenana* once a day to coach Nadira. He taught her across a curtain of silk. Under his tutelage, Nadira's music grew more enchanting. Her favourite *raga* was the *bahaar*.

It was during one of those beautiful spring evenings—the birds chirped sweeter than before and the trees swayed lyrically—that Nadira found a handwritten note slipped inside the pages of her songbook. It had a beautiful sketch of a woman chasing a moon. The inscription underneath read, 'To my Anarkali'.

It was signed. 'Yours, in love. Salim.'

Nadira did not know how the artistic note had come to her, but she was certain that it was meant for her. She recognised the name Salim for she had heard tales of the handsome and rebellious prince and of his paintings. She brought the note closer to her face and smelt the *itr* on the paper. This unforeseen romantic attention and such artistic expression made her happy. Not only was he young and delightfully charming, they said, she felt a connection between her own artistic self and the unusual prince. She had never been courted this way before. Of course, the Emperor desired her. But she had never felt anything for him, only that she had been tasked and asked for her services by the monarch.

When this sudden sweet and serious love beckoned, she did not know how to respond or who to trust to reach out to the prince. She sat in the rose garden, wondering how to communicate her feelings to the prince, mulling over the stakes and the consequences if she were discovered. She finally resorted to seeking advice from the only confidant she had.

'Whenever I hear chronicles of love, they all begin with hesitation, then they develop into an act of submission. All these tales end badly and lovers are left with the anguish of being apart. Is there such a thing as love, a spiritual craving, that destiny truly supports?' she asked Mian sahab during one of their music lessons.

Smiling, his eyes closed, Mian sahab read her mind and responded without looking at her. 'Are you afraid to love, Nadira?'

'I don't know, Mian sahab. I am confused.'

Mian sahab had begun to take a liking to his new student. She was skilful, diligent and a beautiful young girl, almost the same age as his own daughter. His heart ached with fatherly affection when he thought about the miseries of her life. What a life she must have led to land up in the harem for the Emperor's carnal pleasures instead of the comforts of a home. He took a deep long breath and responded.

'There are phases of accepting this ethereal phenomenon called love. First, complacently as a natural state and then, as an anticipated offshoot of a different pursuit, realising what a wonderful thing it is to have happened to you. This is what makes love so delicate and unpredictable. Yes, it is an untamed force that will enslave you. It will leave you fulfilled, yet empty at the same time. Are you ready to be vanquished by your beautiful enemy?'

In that moment as a desperate longing overruled any logic, Nadira slipped in a handful of rose petals into the book and passed it on to Mian sahab. He smiled as he took it away.

Soon this became a ritual. The book of songs became a book of details: sketches, *peepal* leaves, rose petals and love notes. The young lovers grew more impatient by the day, yet they held back in fear, knowing that the ground they were treading on was both dangerous and illicit. If the Emperor found out that his son, the royal heir to the throne of Hindustan, was not only courting a woman of a low social birth but one who was also from his father's harem, it would be tantamount to unpardonable treachery, blasphemy. It could eventually even lead to execution. But it was love and its wild, instinctive and rebellious nature strove against the social scheme of life in Fatehpur Sikri. It was on a fateful spring evening that the two lost the battle and surrendered to each other.

Salim and Anarkali's (for Nadira now loved calling herself by this name) first secret rendezvous, organised and guarded by a handful of trusted allies, took place in a dilapidated horse stable. It was the night of a new moon. They arrived, camouflaged in clothes so ordinary they were unrecognisable. In the darkness of the night, Salim lit a small fire so he could see her face. The lights of the embers, the complete stillness of the hour, the ordinariness of their clothing, the distance from the palace, all of it brought the two soulmates closer to each other.

However, it wasn't before long that the secret was out in the open. Akbar began to hear rumours of the incestuous relationship between his favourite concubine and his son. Later, his spies confirmed that the suspicion was true. In a fit of insane rage, he summoned the two for an explanation. And in his presence, they confessed that they were truly, deeply and miserably in love and unafraid of consequences. Salim, the impertinent crown prince, was ordered to leave Fatehpur Sikri again on another mission to stop a rebellion in the east and Anarkali, his beloved slave girl, was sentenced to be buried alive between walls.

On such a fateful day, Anarkali alias Nadira alias Sharf-un-nisa, the brave, wise, talented and the most beautiful girl in the Emperor's harem, was dragged by her feet in fetters. Masons were ordered to bury her alive.

Only a few bricks remained to close Anarkali's way to her death when the Emperor came to the site of execution. He wanted to ensure that his ruthlessness was held up as an example to all others who served him in the imperial court. He was hoping to see panic and fear in her eyes, but instead, when their eyes met, all he saw was a glint of sunshine. There was no guilt, nor remorse, only an indomitable spirit challenging his might. He hated her at that moment, more than he had when she confessed her love for his son. Frustrated, the Emperor left the site.

What happened next was something neither time nor Anarkali had anticipated. She shut her eyes tight as the last brick closed the wall and realised she would have a few minutes to live before suffocation killed her. Her life flashed before her eyes when she suddenly felt a heavy blow hit on the back of her head and the world behind her came crumbling down. All she saw was an endless tunnel of darkness.

In another part of the Mughal empire, a long caravan was passing through the desert. Its leader, armed with a group of bodyguards in dark robes, was patrolling his rich master's convoy when he suddenly stopped. He stood gaping at the incredible sight before him.

In front of the caravan, right across its path was a woman covered in a thin blanket of sand. Coiled neatly next to her hissed a black hooded cobra. Assuming that the woman had fallen prey to the fury of the merciless desert, the Arab approached. Sensing an impending danger, the serpent moved and raised its glistening head. Its hood shone in the twilight sun. The Arab was a man of the desert and knew instantly that the cobra was the woman's indisputable protector. He stood frozen, unthreateningly, letting the cobra interpret his presence as that of an ally, gently shifting his weight from one foot to the other.

It was unbelievable. As if gauging his fear by his body language, the cobra slowly slithered away into the sand.

The Arab sat down next to the woman, and her red lips began to move. He blew away the sand that covered her beautiful face and watched her angelic features and the tryst of their destinies. He offered her water from his leather bag.

It was time for his evening prayer.

Moving to the side, he unfurled his prayer mat and sat down on the saffron sand, facing Mecca. The woman moved again. Reluctantly, the Arab picked her up and held her against the mellow twilight. Her face glistened in the softened terracotta light, and closing his eyes in prayers, he named her Mehr-un-nisa … the sun among women.

When the woman regained consciousness, she could not recollect how she got there. She had fleeting memories: fear, claustrophobia, walls engulfing her, and then something heavy hitting the back of her head and the walls crumbling around her. A very strong pair of arms had held her before she fell into a deep pit of darkness. The Arab was a god-fearing old man. He took her to be a blessing from Allah, brought her home to his wife and gave her food and shelter. Mehr-un-nisa, with her wise and beautiful demeanour, soon became a part of the family. The old couple began to treat her as their daughter.

In faraway Delhi, Salim, heartbroken, mourned the loss of his soulmate. He then began to plot, focusing on gaining control of the royal throne and consolidating his reign. The artist in him gradually learnt to bury his grief silently in music and art; yet he never forgot Anarkali nor forgave his father. Those who knew him well saw him change. The crown prince was slowly turning into an emperor. After Akbar's death, he took over as the uncontested monarch of Hindustan.

His new name was Emperor Jahangir.

It was a few months after he had assumed his new role that he summoned one of his loyal messengers to his private chamber and gave him a missive.

'In a village bordering the desert, some 500 miles south of Delhi, there is an old Arab who weaves carpets for the imperial mosques. Give him my message and tell him that I wish to see him immediately. Bring him, along with his wife and daughter.' The new Emperor handed the messenger a scroll. 'Go right now.'

When Mehr-un-nisa was told that she had been summoned by the Emperor her heart sank. Memories of a brutal past resurfaced. A man who had once desired her had ordered her death, and the man she had once loved had neither protested nor fought, but had left her to die. Thoughts tormented her but she could not refuse the Emperor.

'Shahenshah Akbar?' she inquired of the messenger.

'No, the newly crowned Emperor of all Hindustan. Jahangir,' the messenger declared.

The Arab, his wife and Mehr-un-nisa were escorted to Delhi to meet the new Emperor. Upon reaching the capital, the Emperor insisted on meeting the daughter alone. 'She will be safe,' the messenger convinced the Arab. 'Emperor Jahangir is a kind-hearted man, unlike his father,' he said and then whispered in the ear of the Arab, 'He is different. He loves flowers, birds, music and art. When he is alone, he paints and sings to himself. Don't worry. He would not harm her.'

Once again, Mehr-un-nisa stepped into the imperial courtyard, her head and face covered by a veil. She was walking alongside her mother when a guard stopped her mother from escorting her any further.

Mehr-un-nisa saw a frightened and hesitant look creep over her foster mother's face and her heart melted. She held her mother's hand and pressed it gently.

'I will be back soon, Ammi. Have faith in Allah.'

With each step towards the Emperor's chamber, her feet felt heavy. '*Who is this Jahangir who wanted to see her alone? Akbar had many sons, so who could this be? Not Salim, for he was almost thrown out of the royal household. But ... was it possible? Had he returned and taken over the throne? Could it be him who summoned her? No, no. Why would he care!*' A million thoughts crossed her mind.

On a marble terrace covered by intricately designed lattice and overlooking a garden of roses, she saw the Emperor standing with his back towards her. A peacock was perched on the *chhatri* over his head. The last rays of the sun fell on him, shadowing a part of his face.

'Shahenshah *huzoor* Jahangir, please accept my salaam,' she bowed to the monarch and he turned to face her.

Time stood still. Mehr-un-nisa froze. Standing in front of her eyes, in the setting light of dusk, with the crown jewel shining on his head, was the Emperor of all Hindustan, the only man she ever loved, Salim. For a few minutes there was only silence between the two; they stood transfixed, looking upon each other, absorbing each other's presence. Believing, disbelieving and yet convincing themselves that this was not a dream. Years of agony disappeared when the Emperor took the first step and pulled Mehr-un-nisa into a warm embrace.

'You left me to die. I thought you didn't care,' she mumbled softly, feeling a stream of tears run down her cheeks.

'How could I not? You were dying for me.' He held her chin and looked into her eyes.

'I still don't know what happened that day. How am I alive?'

'How could I let you die? I found someone to dig a tunnel

under the walls. He helped you escape.'

'Who?'

'Mian sahab. Your teacher.'

'Mian sahab? He was like a father to me. What happened?'

'They were to take you by a safe route to Lahore. But a sandstorm hit the desert, and … I lost you again.'

'Oh my God! That's when my father … he found me.'

'Yes, exactly. My men tracked him down and waited for my orders.'

'And did the Emperor ever find out? Was he not angry? Were you not punished?'

'Yes, he was! He refused to make me his successor.'

'Ya Allah, you risked your life for me?'

'You risked death for me, my love.' His eyes were soft, his embrace tender, and in that moment, she could see the same love that she had found what seemed like a lifetime ago.

'All that is now past, and today, as I stand before you, the Emperor of all Hindustan, Shahenshah Jahangir, I want to proclaim my love for you. Sharf-un-nisa, Nadira, Anarkali, Mehr-un-nisa … whatever the name be, whatever you be, wherever you be, you are and will be the only woman I have ever loved so deeply. Will you marry me?'

Mehr-un-nisa nodded, her affirmations subdued by her cries as she buried her face in his chest and let her love and all its expression escape.

'Welcome home,' he whispered, 'the light of my world, Nur Jahan!'

Moving Shadows

A quiet river
Slivers of shadow
Twigs, marigolds, ashes—
Nomads—all of them,
Floating to salvation.
A fishing net, a bamboo flute
A matchstick and a boatman
A brittle silence
Waiting for a stone.

Moving Shadows

It was almost four-thirty in the morning when Snehil logged out for the day. It was his last conference call with the team in America. The market, already severely impacted by a financial crisis, was about to crash. It could be any time now. Share prices were collapsing fast and global trade was haywire. Speculations transformed to panic.

'It's inevitable now. There has never been a slump like this before. Have you seen the oil prices in the last hour? How can we trade! Unprecedented times, guys. Watch out and buck up!' A tone of desperation was evident in his manager, Bob's, voice.

'Shit!' Snehil swore and wheeled his chair away from the laptop on the dining table, pushing away hard. The back of his chair hit a French buffet sideboard, and toppled down a framed photograph of him, Rashi and Vihaan. He picked up the frame quickly, felt guilty and put it back in its place. It was a lovely family photograph of the three in Disneyland, Hong Kong. Vihaan had thrown a tantrum about revisiting Disneyland for the umpteenth time before they moved to Singapore. Like always, Rashi had taken his side and a reluctant Snehil had to agree to spending a full day with Mickey Mouse and Simba. They moved to Singapore within a few weeks after that.

It was sudden, a golden career opportunity. That is how Bob had described it prior to the move. The Singapore office had needed to replace a senior trader and Bob had recommended his name. Unprepared for the sudden change, Snehil had asked for some time, but Bob pushed him. 'If you don't take it now, someone else will. Don't worry about accommodation or schooling. Singapore is very well equipped. They'll put you up in a serviced apartment until you find a home and move. I am sure your wife and son will love the city and the house.'

With less than a month to prepare, they had moved lock, stock and barrel. And Bob was right. His company had made arrangements for a temporary stay at an extremely plush serviced apartment overlooking the river. The view was stunning. Rashi and Vihaan loved this new city and were settling in quickly. Rashi had even begun to place her personal effects in the apartment and it felt like home. She was the one who had put the photograph there. But it was Snehil who was taking longer than usual to adjust to the new city, the new environment and their home. It had a strange vibe, he felt.

And now that this financial crisis was stealthily creeping up on him, Snehil felt more strongly that a shadow was closing in on his life. A crisis of this scale would dent the business with a substantial loss and burn his own pockets in a way he hadn't remotely imagined. If the market crashed and share prices continued to slide, he would lose a huge chunk of his personal investments, and the thought made him very restless. His mouth went dry.

He stood up and poured himself a glass of cold water. Then he paced up and down the living room and peeped into their bedroom. Rashi was fast asleep on her side of the bed. A soft light from behind the curtains fell on her face. She looked calm and lovely. He didn't want to disturb her so he shut the door quietly. Next, he checked Vihaan's room. Vihaan had a habit of moving like a compass needle in his sleep. Rashi and Snehil often joked about Vihaan needing a circular bed. In those early years, when Vihaan would sneak into the bed with them and refuse to leave, he would move all night, in every possible direction, sometimes even throwing his poor parents off the bed. The memory made Snehil smile. He pulled Vihaan's duvet up to cover him well and tiptoed out of the room.

Snehil was exhausted, but there was no point in trying to sleep any more. The Asian markets would open in only a few hours and his mind was too perturbed to rest. He stood at the large window overlooking the river and wondered why he hadn't spent more time admiring the gorgeous skyline of his new country of residence. It wasn't dawn yet, and the nightscape was dotted by a million lights, shimmering soaring skyscrapers in the Central Business District, gently kissing the spires and bell towers of old churches, mysteriously lighting up tall pillars of grand colonial buildings and hiding the alleys of red-roofed traditional shophouses like a little secret. A million other lights glistened on the reflection in the river. It was as if a fairy's magic wand had touched a painting with a sparkler and it had miraculously come alive.

Snehil looked at his watch again. It was five in the morning.

'There isn't much that I can do now until the Asian markets open. Too little time to catch a nap, too much to waste in a panic anticipating doom. I can go for a run, perhaps. The fresh air will do me good,' he thought aloud. Not wanting to disturb or wake Rashi, he picked up a pair of shorts and a tee from the clothes line, changed into his running shoes and left home.

Snehil took a little turn as he stepped out of the gate, taking the road along the river. The streets were barren and there wasn't another person in sight. Intriguing shapes of light and shadow lined the road, making a maze-like pattern on the path in front of him. A thin mist hung over him. Snehil realised it was still very early for joggers and runners in this part of the island. He, of course, didn't miss their company. The fresh morning air felt good against his tired body, the endorphins somewhat reducing the stress he felt at that moment. But still, Snehil kept oscillating between nothingness and the impending danger of a crisis befalling his life.

It was like he wasn't seeing where he was running and he didn't care.

However, in that hazy and somewhat blinding moment of psychological stress, something caught Snehil's eyes and he froze. From a distance, through the layers of the morning mist, his eyes fell on a large tree by the river. Something hung from its branches and from this distance, they looked human. As Snehil rubbed his eyes and tried to focus, he saw the bodies. Several human dead bodies were tied upside down, hanging from the tree. Their eyes were all transfixed in his direction.

Snehil's first instinct was to turn around and run home, but an overwhelming fear gripped him. He wanted to shout, but he had lost his voice; his throat had dried up and his body felt heavy. He couldn't move an inch. He turned away, shutting his eyes tightly, rationalising in his mind that this was impossible.

First of all, there could be no dead bodies hanging like that from a tree in a city as modern and safe as Singapore. Secondly, it was impossible that they were all looking at him.

Then he started running. The fastest run he had ever made. It wasn't until he had run for at least a couple of minutes with his eyes tight shut that he opened them again. A purple streak of light flashed through the dark sky, followed by dark magenta, then orange. In a few minutes, as he headed homewards, the sky turned a gilded yellow. Soon, streaks of blue fell through the gaps in the moving shadows of the clouds towering over the island. The sun was just beginning to break its way into dawn.

Rashi was already up and sitting in the living room in her pyjamas. The door was wide open, and she seemed anxious. She ran to meet him as he stepped out of the elevator.

'Where on earth were you?' She threw a volley of questions at him. 'You didn't come to bed last night? And you left home without telling me. I called you so many times. Why can't you carry your phone? Do you even know how sick I have been with worry since I woke up?'

'Sorry, I … forgot my phone. I … erm… just went for a run,' Snehil mumbled.

'Are you okay? You look pale. What's wrong, Snehil?'

'Nothing. I am okay. Just stressed, I think.'

'Are you sure? You look like you have seen a ghost!'

There, she said it first! Snehil held Rashi tight and broke into a hysteric bout of incoherent self-doubt. He cried, 'I don't know what I saw, Rashi, but I swear … on Vihaan … I saw those dead bodies hanging from the tree. They were all looking straight at me. Rashi, something terrible is happening … something terrible will happen to us …'

Rashi tried to calm him down, attributing the hallucination to stress at work.

'Love, ghosts don't exist. You know it. I know it. You are

an engineer. You studied science, remember? This is all in your mind. I have read so much about visions and hallucinations manifesting from stress. It must be that. There are no ghosts. You are just exhausted. You haven't slept or eaten for hours. The body and brain react to such negligence. You have been working too hard. This upheaval in the financial market is burning you out, I tell you. I think you should take a day off and tell Bob that you need the rest. Your brain needs to unplug.'

As Snehil retold what he had seen, his vision and its interpretation sounded ludicrous to his own ears. He wanted to agree with Rashi and dismiss the thought. But the image was etched on his mind.

Rashi and Snehil agreed to put a lid on the incident and move on. A few weeks later, Rashi finally found the house of her dreams. Their sea-facing apartment was right in the Indian part of town and it was all that they could ask for. It meant new friends, a good social life and some space to de-stress from their workload. Snehil and Rashi began to see a strong ray of hope that their lives would change for the better. They picked the next weekend as the red-letter day to move.

On D-day, since they didn't have too many boxes, and the freight from Hong Kong had already reached their new home, the family decided to divide the move into two shifts. Snehil and Vihaan left early with a taxi full of suitcases and bags. Rashi stayed back to ensure that the serviced apartment was well cleaned before handing the keys over to the management staff. Once the formalities were done, Rashi called a taxi and left. She gave the cabbie her new address.

'Do you live here?' the old cabbie asked her.

'I used to, Uncle. Now we are moving to the address I gave

you,' she replied promptly.

'Ah, the ghetto! That area is full of expats like you. You will like it there. This one is an old part of Singapore.'

It was a busy Saturday afternoon and the traffic was slow. 'Did you like staying here?' the man asked, wanting to keep the conversation going. Rashi replied non-committally with a curt 'Yes'.

'I see. Not many people like to stay here,' the cabbie continued.

The strange statement took Rashi by surprise and she looked up inquiringly. 'What do you mean, Uncle? Why?'

'This place has a history, you see.'

'What history? Can you tell me about it?' Rashi asked curiously.

'Well, back in those days during the Second World War, the Japanese invaded Singapore. Do you know about it?'

'Yes, I have read about it,' Rashi responded promptly.

'Books don't tell you everything, *lah*.' She caught his smile in the mirror.

'I know. But I have heard about the Japanese attack on Alexandra Hospital.'

'Yes, that was one of the worst. I was just born that year, so I have no memory of this, but I used to hear from my dad that large troops of Japanese soldiers attacked the hospital. They went from room to room, killing patients, doctors, nurses. Everyone they saw. They say some hundred people were held captive, but all were executed in the end. You can check on the internet.'

'Right, I will.' Rashi grew more interested in this history lesson.

'Many atrocities took place, many common people suffered,'

the cabbie continued, even as the taxi was nearing Rashi's new home. 'The *kempeitai*, or the military police brutally carried out a *sook ching*, meaning a purging—to get rid of the ethnic Chinese population. The massacre, they say, killed over 50,000 ethnic Chinese here in Singapore and in Malaysia.'

'Oh gosh! That's insane. So many people?' On seeing the house, Rashi felt impatient but she decided to listen to the rest of the story before alighting from the cab.

'Yes, they say the victims were mostly male, between eighteen and fifty years old. They were all rounded up, taken to deserted spots and then executed. Later, just for all to see and fear the Japanese in their hearts, they hung the dead bodies. They strung them up near the area where you lived, and left them upside down on trees along the river.'

Note

This is based on a true story. The names of the characters have been changed to protect privacy.

Petrichor

'Here's my passport and ticket, and the other documents.' I choked as I handed my travel documents across the counter to the airline staff. The woman looked up at me, squinted through her glasses, nonchalantly leafed through the sheets and paused.

'Oh, I am so sorry!' Her voice was gentle. 'Please wait.'

She got up and left to 'discuss the case' with a senior staff member. There were a few people in uniform and name tags, and they looked at me with an expression of empathy and suspicion. One of them was kind enough to offer me a seat, a glass of water and to ask if I was okay.

No, I was not! My fiancé was dead. And with him, a part of my life had just been blown into a million pieces.

It was one of the worst terrorist attacks on the United States of America, a country we had both begun to love as our own, where we had wanted to settle in soon.

It had been too sudden and shocking. I could not believe it was real. I mean, this was the sort of thing that only happened in movies and always to somebody else, right?

Yes, you could say I was still living in denial.

Adi and I had been seeing each other for almost two years now, and he had proposed with a fake diamond ring only two weeks ago. It was over a few tequila shots, right here in Times Square, in the middle of the night. He had declared his undying love for me and asked me to marry him. I thought that the idiot was stressed because of his workload, dead drunk and joking. He swore he wasn't. He also promised he would be mine and stay by my side in sickness and health for the rest of our lives.

I cannot say if I was really in love or even if I was ready to marry him, but the junkie with all his charms convinced me that I would eventually consider him worthy. With some hesitation, I heard myself saying 'Yes'.

And now he was gone. Just like that! Without a warning or a word. He had been simply obliterated from the face of the earth, blown into a hundred pieces of flesh and gore. I realised that I was still wearing the ring. Yes, the fake one. Now it would never have the chance to transform into a real rock. Much like my commitment.

Everything had happened too soon.

I wasn't feeling well and had chosen to work from home on that fateful day. Adi had, of course, left home early that morning to get to work on time. We spoke while he was heading out, and he insisted we talk to his father and inform him about the engagement. It could not have been more than a few hours when I walked down to a coffee shop in the neighbourhood I frequented.

Alice, the elderly lady at the counter, knew me well from my habitual coffee pangs and was usually very nice to her customers. But she paid no attention to me that morning. Her eyes were glued to the TV. It looked like a familiar shot of Manhattan, but something was strange about it.

'What film is this?' I asked.

Alice shook her head and said, 'No, it's real, love. Someone's flown a plane into the tower.'

Soon the entire coffee shop had gathered in front of the screen—all jaws dropped as the audience stood wide-eyed and silent. I heard Alice screaming. 'Jesus Christ! It's going! It's going!' And as we looked, we watched the first tower fall. Yes, it was that quick and that simple! It only took a few fanatic minds and the seamless execution of a devilish plan to ravage my life, and that of hundreds of others who perished on 9/11. And here I was, sitting in an airport lounge, struggling to find an airline that would agree to ship a coffin, clueless about what state of mind I should be in. I didn't know whether I should be in mourning or be practical and brave as I carried pieces of Adi, the remains of whatever they could find in the debris, to his dad in Mauritius.

Brigadier Awadhoot Kaul and I had spoken on the phone on the night of the disaster. I found his number on a little yellow sticky note on the refrigerator: 'In case of emergency.' I had spent countless hours teasing Adi about what a daddy's little boy he was, running to his father for everything, despite being a thirty-year-old. Adi was raised single-handedly by his superhero dad ever since his mother passed away when he was a child.

'You will love the old man when you meet him. He is nothing like me. More your type. Organised, brave and pragmatic like you. He even listens to the same kind of music you love … the kind that puts me to sleep!' He would joke. I had never imagined that one day I would, in fact, need to use that number and to make an emergency call.

The conversation with Adi's father was not easy, but I must admit, he was braver than all of Adi's stories combined. Maybe it was because he was a retired army officer, or maybe because he had lost his wife early in life. But he spoke in an expressionless voice and asked me if I would be kind enough to send the coffin over or to escort it to Mauritius. He would pay for my travel, he insisted. 'I will be there at the airport. I would like it very much if you escort my boy home in his last journey and not leave him to the mercy of the airport staff. They did not know him. You did,' he said firmly.

I had become a part of the many lives that were devastated by the terrorist attack on America. Much as I was upset about my fiancé's untimely death, I wasn't quite sure if I wanted to do this. I felt strange that the man I never had a chance to fall in love with was taking over my life after his death. I felt the need to mourn, but it was the despair, darkness and loss of the entire nation that overwhelmed me. Condolence messages were pouring in from friends and colleagues and the social circle we had built around ourselves, yet I felt guilty that I was not true. I wasn't Adi's lover, and had hardly been a fiancée for more than a few days. I decided to speak to my mother. Over a long-distance call, I explained, 'I know I should be sad, and trust me, I am. Adi's death has shaken me, just as death has shaken the families and friends of all those who died, but I would feel no differently if it were another friend. I mean, I am affected, but I don't feel that my world has come to an end. I am quite ... okay, erm I mean ... actually, clinically managing and learning to move on.'

Ma heard me patiently, as only she could, and asked, 'Are you feeling guilty?'

'I don't know, Ma. I just don't feel like a widow.'

'You are not!' she said sharply.

'But I am expected to be in mourning. Friends and colleagues are drowning me with sympathy. I almost feel that I am faking. That's not right. I have never pretended. Adi knew it as well. I didn't promise him anything that was not real, even in our commitment. Our relationship was very transparent. We were friends giving ourselves a chance to be a couple. I am not being insensitive. I am sad, but I am not dead. I just feel like I am being a hypocrite, cheating myself and Adi like this.'

'I don't see a reason why you should feel this way. You are being honest to yourself. Yes, it is shocking and saddening, but if you are not depressed, you simply aren't. You don't have to feel guilty. You have never lived for the gallery and Adi loved you for that. Why would you let pretensions creep into your life now after his death?'

'Ma, I know. But what if his dad expects a mourning widow?'

'What if he doesn't? Let us not presume anything. We don't know him. If you are worried about escorting the coffin, I think you should go. You are a responsible adult who cares that her friend died in a merciless disaster; you should make sure that the deceased reaches his own home. If you put aside your dilemma, that's the right thing to do. Just don't stay there too long.'

'I understand what you are saying. Love you, Ma.' I hung up, having found my answer.

The long flight to Port Louis, Mauritius, was uneventful. Every time I remembered that I was carrying Adi's coffin with me, I felt a lump in my throat and my eyes started to burn. I tried to watch a film or read a book, but my mind kept going back to a strange cusp between sadness and practicality. I popped in a light sedative and slept through most of the flight. The airline staff were particularly nice, and I imagined that they were briefed about the 'personal loss' and the 'baggage' I was carrying.

I recognised Brigadier Kaul at the airport from the photographs I had seen of him. Tall, lean and extremely fit for his age, he looked very much the 'commando super dad' as Adi had described him. He was wearing a white linen shirt and a pair of denims. His face had the perfect proportions of courage and calm, much like anyone who had seen enough war and death in his life. An indescribable emotion lingered in his eyes and his jaws tightened as he saw the dark wooden box behind me. I pushed the trolley to where he stood and found myself standing in front of him. We said nothing to each other. Not a word. No shaking of hands, no exchange of pleasantries. Just a silent conversation when our eyes met. For a brief second, I thought I saw him swallow his agony. He signalled to four men to lift the coffin into a funeral van. I followed them to the vehicle.

Adi's funeral was quiet. There was no crying, not even a loud whisper or wail. There were only a handful of other people, who I assumed were family friends, mostly dressed in white. They stared at me with pathos. One of them passed a bottle of water over. No one spoke except for the priest who was chanting some *mantra*s and directing Adi's dad to perform the last rites. I hadn't been to a funeral before and the finality of the ritual, the burning pyre and the stillness of the surroundings made me wonder about the ephemeral significance of our material lives.

It was only on the drive back from the crematorium that Brigadier Kaul spoke to me for the first time since I had landed.

'How was your flight?' he asked as he began to drive.

'It was good, thank you!'

'You must be very tired. You can take a shower, have dinner and rest when we reach home.' His voice had a softness I hadn't felt in the last couple of hours.

I managed a faint grateful smile and said, 'Thank you.'

The house of Brigadier Kaul was a dream: a villa straight out of a travel magazine. After his retirement from the armed forces in India, he had relocated to Mauritius and bought a beautiful colonial-style villa in the foothills of a mountain. It faced the aquamarine sea. The spectacular villa was ambushed in a green canopy and tucked amidst the dense floral abundance of scarlet red clusters of the flame of the forest and white orchids. Far from the pandemonium and urban chaos, the softly lit timeless acre of land was named 'Petrichor', the fragrance of the earth after the first rain. In Adi's stories of his dad, Petrichor outlined and encapsulated the soul of the land on which the house was built.

On a little plaque beside the wooden gate—a pleasure since I hated iron doors—the name was inscribed, and it shone under the light of a yellow lamp carved out of the bark of a tree. The dimly lit garden patterned the dark foliage. I noticed a signboard that indicated this was the last cottage bordering the Black River Gorges National Park. The red-brick wall porch had been converted into a cosy sitting area by strategically hanging glass lanterns and placing potted palms in ceramic and terracotta basins. It looked like an idyllic spot to spend quiet afternoons sketching, taking a nap or simply observing the ocean and the movements of plants and animals.

Brigadier Kaul noted my awed, Alice-in-wonderland expression, and said, 'You can spend some time looking around tomorrow. It's a beautiful country.'

'Hmm,' I said and added, 'Thank you.'

'You don't have to thank me for everything. I should be the one thanking you for bringing my boy home.' His voice softened again at the mention of his son, and I looked away. I saw the living room resplendent with well-chosen artefacts, old family photographs on the mantel, a decorated silver frame of a beaming Adi from his university convocation, souvenirs of a world traveller, brass mementoes and trophies, and memoirs of another life in the Indian army.

'So I'll see you at dinner ... do you have any dietary restrictions?'

'No, I am good. Thank you ...' I said and bit my tongue. 'See you.' I thought I saw a faint smile cross his face as I walked away.

At dinner, which was simple Indian fare of chapaati, steamed rice, rajma, matar paneer, raita and salad, we did not once mention Adi.

'Sorry about the vegetarian fare. I am not religious, but my cook doesn't make non-vegetarian food these days. I have tried to reason with him and to tell him that it's been a few weeks since ... but he has his own beliefs.'

'No problem at all. I love rajma.' I poured a bowlful of the brown curry into my rice. I was famished; the last meal I had had was on the flight, several hours ago.

'That's unusual for a Bengali.'

'Yes, my Ma tells me I am a Kashmiri soul trapped in a Bengali body.'

'Is it? Do you have a connection?'

'I was born in Jammu and spent my early childhood in Jammu and Jyotipuram. I have a soft spot for anything Kashmiri.'

'Ah, I see. I was raised in Srinagar, but of course, we had to move out when the Kashmiri Pandits were evicted ...'

He enquired about my parents and my career and then asked me how long I wanted to stay in Mauritius. 'Sorry about asking, and you can stay here if you want to, but I need to know when you've decided to return to New York. I need to arrange the logistics.'

'Oh sure. I should have already mentioned this. I have a flight tomorrow evening.'

I thanked him for the meal, wished him goodnight and headed to the guest room. Before I retired for the night, I faintly heard the lyrics of one of my favourite ghazals by Mehdi Hassan playing somewhere in the house.

Kis kis ko batayenge judaai ka sabab hum
Tu mujhse khafa hai to zamaane ke liye aa.

Who else must I explain the reason of separation?
Come, despite your displeasure, to continue the ceremony.

I slept like a log that night as soon as I turned in. When I woke up the next morning, it took me a while to register where I was. From the windows facing the garden, I could see the early morning sunlight playing on the leaves, teasing the swaying branches of the flame of the forest. A soft mist was rising from the moist earth, still bathed in dewdrops, looming like a mysterious dream over the landscape. I felt a sudden burst of enthusiasm, something I hadn't felt in the gloom and despair of post-9/11 America. I picked up my sneakers and walked out of Petrichor.

The road ahead meandered uphill to almost touch the sky,

and was camouflaged by tall equatorial trees. My curiosity took me to the end of the winding stretch, and I found that it rolled out to a seemingly endless cul-de-sac. I walked up right till the edge of the inestimable road to nowhere to look at the glowing dawn across the National Park. 'I didn't know you were a sunrise person too,' a voice called out.

'Good morning,' I said, recognising Adi's father.

'Morning,' he responded and walked up to me.

'Do you come here often?' I asked, resting on a piece of rock.

'Yes, every day.'

'For the sunrise?'

'Yes, it is a delightful sight to see the sun shear its way through the dark curtains of the night sky.'

'Wow! You are also very poetic.' I smiled at him.

'While it may be repetitive, to me it is like seeing a painting come alive. Look at that bold vermilion across the clouds, tipping over the hill?' He pointed and I added to his scene. 'And how the scarlet has spilled generously over the valley, right up to the sea! This is so amazing. I am missing my camera.'

'Are you fond of photography too? I have nurtured some love for this new interest recently. You can check my cameras if you want.'

'Really? I saw some stunning photographs in your home. You are Nat Geo material.'

He seemed embarrassed. 'Well ... yes, but I don't think they are that good. Thank you.' I noticed a dimple on his right cheek as he smiled.

I asked him about the photograph of a strange-looking mountain I had spotted in his living room. 'A round rock sat on another big rock like the ultimate balancing act. Together, they looked like a young man,' I said. 'That's Pieter Both,' he explained. 'According to folklore, a young milkman once lived on this island. One day, when he was walking to a house, it started to rain. So, he took shelter behind a rock. He eventually fell asleep and woke up to song. When he opened his eyes, he found fairies singing and dancing in front of him. The leader of the fairies said, "You are special to be able to see us, but you shall not tell anyone about this or you will be turned to stone". But the fairy was not heeded, and the next day, when he went to the top of a mountain and told everyone what he had seen, he turned to stone. It is said that if you look from afar at the mountain, you will see a big rock which is the young boy's head. So, we must keep our promises or become stones.'

The story enraptured me. He asked me again if I wanted to see Mauritius. 'It might sound a little insensitive, but I am not sure you will come back to this lovely island ever again. What we have lost is gone, and what we have, can never be taken from us. You might as well go out and look around a bit.'

My perception of Brigadier Kaul had changed completely in the last twenty-four hours since I had arrived. He was no longer the mourning father of my ex-fiancé, a man I was afraid would judge me for being somewhat nonchalant and overly clinical. I knew how close Adi had been to his dad, and now I knew how unlike each other they were. No wonder Adi always told me I would have liked him. Here was a man who despite his own agonies had not spent a minute displaying them and was instead trying to appreciate everyday life. I felt a strange attachment to him and I wished I had known him earlier.

A storm hit the island that day and all my plans came to a halt. Heavy rains lashed against the walls and the sea seemed enraged. There wasn't much I could do; I spent the entire day wandering around the house and discovered a beautiful library in the attic. It had wooden shelves stacked with books. Khaled Hosseini, Richard Bach, Paulo Coelho, Jeffrey Archer, Salman Rushdie, Roald Dahl, Agatha Christie, and Sir Arthur Conan Doyle. What struck me beyond the impressive collection was that it seemed as if someone had made a photocopy of my imaginary wish list of books and filled the space with everything that I had ever wanted to read. It could not have been Adi! He never read anything beyond the headlines of the newspaper and the sports page.

Then I found *Jonathan Livingston Seagull*, my favourite book on the shelves and got so excited that I rushed downstairs to tell Brigadier Kaul. Our interests were so similar it was uncanny. I found him sitting in the living room with his eyes closed. He looked slightly older than when I last saw him this morning. Mehdi Hassan's mellifluous voice echoed across the room…

Ek umr se hoon lazzat e girya se bhi mehruum
Aye raahat e jaan mujhko rulaane ke liye aa

Too long have I been deprived of the pathos of longing;
Come my love, if only to make me weep again.

Affection filled my heart. Had I met him on any another day or in another place, I knew he would be the man I could have so naturally fallen in love with. I decided to let him sleep, wrote a note thanking him for everything and left it on the coffee table before I left Petrichor. Coincidentally, the earth was smelling of sweet rain as I walked out of the wooden gate.

The taxi driver who picked me up looked at me suspiciously

and after I had settled in a bit asked, 'You don't live there. Are you a relative?'

'Well, yes and no. Do you know them?'

'Who doesn't? Such a tragedy! The poor boy was killed in 9/11, and the doting Brigadier died almost immediately in shock. Such paternal affection!'

'What are you talking about?'

'Everybody around knows, madam. It's been two weeks since. That's why I am surprised to pick you up from here. They don't have any relatives around here. And there is no son any more. We cremated the father ourselves.'

His voice trailed off as my head began to spin … where had I been. In that state of semi-consciousness, I could still hear the fading lines of my favourite ghazal …

Pehle se maraasim na sahi phir bhi kabhi to
Rasm-o-rahe duniya hi nibhaane ke liye aa

If not for our past association
Come to fulfil the rituals of the world.

The Masks

It is well past midnight and I am unable to sleep. I can't hear a single whisper in the wind outside my window. It is as if the night is speechless, mourning the death of every victim of every genocide on this day with silence, until the minutes add up to hours of a pervasive, dark and muffled reticence.

I reach out for my phone to check the time. It's forty past twelve in the morning and I am beginning to feel restless, shifting from side to side, changing the angle of my pillow and wondering if I should just get up and pop in a pill to fight one of my worst enemies after claustrophobia—insomnia. I pour myself a glass of water and decide against medication. I close my eyes again and try to focus on sleep. All I see through the dark filters of the night are electric blue lines and orange waves floating in a purplish pattern, almost like a graphic animation in a tech show reel. My mind is hyperactive and refuses to calm down.

I unspool my thoughts. I console myself and in a self-disciplining voice dictate, 'Stop thinking, just go off to sleep.' I don't wish to be typecast as an idiosyncratic scatterbrain, sieving the nuisances from the worthy, not at this hour of the night.

And then I hear a soft hollow laughter.

Am I hearing voices, I wonder! It's unlikely that I am hallucinating because I am so wide awake.

I strain to hear it … yes, I hear it again. This time it is a hollow muffled guffaw. And it's a male voice. It's impossible that a neighbour could be awake at this hour and laughing out loud. And the laughter is so hushed, barely audible, like someone has cracked a very private joke amongst a group of very close friends. What's uncanny is that it seems close, not more than a few hands away. Is it a trespasser? The feeling is eerie, but I muster the courage to leave my bed and follow the laughter.

As I walk past the dining room, now bathed in a soft yellow light, the laughter suddenly stops. It is as if someone has gotten wind of my arrival and is expressing his or her disapproval at my invasion. Then I see her.

She is sitting on the edge of the couch, her knees folded, and her mermaid-like body is turned at an awkward angle towards my antique His Master's Voice gramophone. A dim light is falling on the waves of her hair. From what I can see, she is brown, very brown. I have seen her before, but I cannot recall where. She looks up at me and smiles.

'Who the hell are…' I am ready to charge at her.

'Shhh, don't speak.' She stops me with an authority that surprises me. It is as if I am an intruder in her house and not the other way around.

For a moment, I am captivated by the artistry of the locks of her hair, almost hypnotised by the sheer beauty and uniqueness of my unusual guest. 'Who are you? What on earth are you doing in my living room at this unearthly hour?' I protest in a whisper.

'You don't know me?' She throws back the question at me,

almost disappointed that I have failed her.

'Am I supposed to?' I rack my brains trying to remember.

'Yes, we met in Barcelona, by the sea. You had your eyes set on me the moment you saw me. Or so you said. Then you brought me home,' she speaks softly.

It is only when she says Barcelona that a bell rings. How I love that vibrant beautiful city, and then I remember how hers was the only face that had stood out amidst a thousand others.

'Goodness! But you … you are not real! How can you be? And you are not supposed to be here. I put you up on the … wall in the dining room. How can you be here?' I shout in disbelief!

'Shh … don't be so loud. It's the middle of the night. You will wake everyone.' She puts a delicate finger on her lips, silencing me. 'I know you are surprised. Anyone in your place would be. This is my little secret. In fact, our little secret! Every night, when you retire from the long hard day's work and fall asleep, we come alive …'

'Now, who is we?' I don't understand her.

'All of us … the masks you wear and the ones you don't, and the ones you have so proudly displayed on the walls.' I hear a soft chorus from my favourite sunshine orange wall, decorated with many many masks.

This is where the different spirits from across the world meet. In my home. Wood, brass, yak bone and papier mâché; ribbon-tied, red, blue, gold, sometimes in batik finish. I have hand-picked and painstakingly collected these masks from wherever I have travelled across the globe. Some of them are dramatic portraits of spirits, departed ancestors of forgotten African tribes, some have a religious or spiritual identity, whilst others are theatrical, symbolic and mysterious. And each one of them is special, because there is a culture, a tradition and a secret behind all the hollow eyes and mouths.

However, I am intrigued by the revelation of this regular, non-inclusive but private meeting in my own home! And if I must admit, I am upset.

'Really? So, what do you gather to discuss behind my back every night?'

The Korean theatre mask with the biggest smile and two strands of black braided hair on either side of his bald head starts to chuckle. 'We bitch about your guests and debate over the men you must see and the funny bunch of hypocrites you call friends.'

'Shut up,' his insolence grates on me.

'Oh, are you insecure?' he asks.

'No. Why should I be? But how dare you, you are but a formless head! How dare you insult my friends?' I retort immediately at the impertinent jester.

'Chuck, stop!' A deep-throated voice resonates from another corner of the wall. I notice the mouth of the chief of the Ashanti tribe move.

'Yes, your highness.' The mask obliges.

'Who is Chuck?' I am curious that they even have nicknames!

'That idiot who opens his mouth so wide that his brains fall out,' responds another voice from the top of the wall. I see the hollow of the mouth of the vicious-looking Tibetan Mahakaal mask. The big off-white canines are shining in the soft light of the lamp, like fangs of a deadly snake. It's one of the ugliest in my collection, and I sometimes wonder if it can really ward off the evil eye as it is meant to.

He spots the rejection in my face immediately and as if reading the thoughts in my mind, continues ...

'Tibetans are characterised by our red faces and history is witness to this truth. Did you know that the troops of the Tubo kingdom painted their faces with blood to terrorise the enemy? In our culture, red masks represent bravery, intelligence and the skill to use strategy to conquer or advise others.'

'Really? Tell me more.' I don't like its face but am impressed by its insight. I decide to sit on the floor, facing the wall, listening to the whispers of the night.

The Ashanti chief speaks again. 'Unlike you humans, we respect courage. From where I and several of my fellow Africans come, every mask has a traditional or spiritual meaning.'

'I didn't know that. Tell me about it,' I enquire like a keen student.

'Conceptually ...' he clears his throat and carries on. 'The wearer of the ritual mask surrenders his human identity and transforms into the spirit represented by the mask. He then becomes a medium for dialogue between the spirit and the community. Also, traits representing moral values are found in masks.'

'What kind of traits?' I ask.

'Masks from the Senefou people of the Ivory Coast have their eyes half closed, symbolising a peaceful attitude, self-control and patience. In Sierra Leone, the small eyes and mouth represent modesty, whilst a wide, protruding forehead represents wisdom. In Gabon, large chins and mouths represent authority and strength. Round eyes may represent alertness and anger, and a straight nose represents unwillingness to retreat.' I turn to focus on my masks from Gabon, assessing them with my newly acquired knowledge. They look unperturbed.

I hear a yawn and look up to see my Indonesian batik couple stretch their facial muscles. 'If you are done asking these unromantic questions, can I ask you for a favour?' The woman speaks to me.

'Yes, of course!'

'Can you move me to his left? I am bored with being on the right and seeing only this part of him.'

I stand up and oblige to enable a change of perspective. I think I see the male counterpart smile with a wink.

My eyes begin to search for the quieter ones now. What's their story? Does the red Chinese mask with golden painted eyes have a Cantonese mystery to share? What about the Arabian ones with gilded bodies? Does the Vietnamese mask carved out of a tree root know where it came from, and what is the history of the beaded one from Ghana? What war stories of the jungle does the Masai tribal king know? Does he miss home? And the bejewelled shell mask from Mauritius, the yak bone Garuda and Ganesha from the Himalayan kingdom of Nepal, and that old green tree Welsh man … do they feel claustrophobic? Do these masks communicate more than I know? Do they know each other's countries, cultures and languages? The Cambodian Buddha stares at me with a serene grimness. His look is laced with a quiet allegation. His eyes are closed in meditation. They seem to speak to me: 'My renunciation of domestic life is meaningless if you buy me off the shelves from expensive home décor boutiques, bring me back to the confines of your plush homes, frame me or nail me to your walls like a piece of tastefully acquired property. I, who had left the material world for a spiritual journey, have been able to teach you nothing.'

I don't know how long I have been asleep. A light rain screens through the open windows, spraying droplets of restless dreams on my face and hair. When I wake up, I find myself lying on the carpet, facing the bright orange wall. All the masks that were so alive last night are silent now. It is as if they have lost their tongues, or like they had never spoken.

I begin to gather myself up, unable to comprehend if I was awake or dreaming last night when my eyes fall on a soft brown piece of a fine fabric. I reach out and pick it up.

No, wait!

It is not plain fabric; it feels like peeled off skin ... and it has the imprint of a nose, a lip and two hollows of the eyes. Is it mine?

Of Stars,
Planets and Boundaries

The answer, my friend, is in everything
that I have not told you yet...

Fakira

With its pink sandstone minarets and mosques, quaint bazaars buzzing with the ancient charm of antique silver and spice, fragrance of argan oil, bejewelled horse-drawn carriages and camel carts, pastilla and tagine stalls, merchants in flowing robes and women in black burqas and beautiful embroidered *djellabas* rustling through the narrow lanes and souks, the fortified city of Marrakesh looked like a page from a travel magazine.

I had always wanted to see it, so when life offered me an opportunity to visit Morocco, I took it. It was my chance to live the traveller's dream in one of the world's oldest civilisations, tucked far away between the Atlantic and the Mediterranean, breathing in a bit of Arabia, Europe and Africa. And now that I was here, it felt like I had been absorbed into a landscape from the Arabian Nights and had become a part of the past.

'Morocco is a mystic and a magician. You can almost see the country as a young fakir, draping his modesty, spirituality and wisdom all in an old-world charm,' my driver-cum-guide, Zafar, stated philosophically as we entered the busiest parts of the bustling pink-walled city, hemmed in by the swaying palm trees. It was almost time for lunch and I was dying to taste the much-acclaimed cuisine before delving into the depths of the city's history, philosophy and culture. 'If you want to eat Moroccan food, you must eat couscous and lamb tagine,' Zafar recommended. Fortunately, we found a good restaurant nearby and settled for the menu Zafar had suggested. Needless to say, the taste was beyond words.

Next, I wanted to pick up some antique silver and leather trinkets. We began to walk through the meandering alleys of the erstwhile imperial city, soaking up its medieval history, while Zafar explained the long and chequered past of the country, the influence of the French, the fakirs and the most recent impact of tourism on Marrakesh.

'I don't know if you are aware, Marrakesh is also known as the Red or Ochre City because of the pink/red sandstone walls and the buildings. Ali Ibn Yusuf built the city in the twelfth century and it grew rapidly as a cultural, religious and trading hub,' he elaborated. Whilst his natural flair for storytelling kept me engaged, I wanted to tell him that I had done my homework and read about Marrakesh already. He was telling me things I already knew and I wanted to tell him things that he didn't know. 'These pink sandstone walls remind me of an Indian town, Jaipur in Rajasthan,' I said, looking around at the city walls.

'Really?' He was curious, so I showed him photographs from a recent trip to Jaipur to attend a literature festival, when I had taken some time off to visit the proverbial Pink City. After seeing a few photographs of the Hawa Mahal and the camels, he was convinced that the two cities looked similar.

'The world is a curious place, you see! Who would have imagined Marrakesh had a twin in India?' Zafar laughed and guided me to a quieter nook. 'You see, at the beginning of the seventeenth century, Marrakesh grew very popular among Sufi pilgrims, and seven of the patron saints of Morocco are buried here. Some of the pilgrims still come here often. See that fakir?'

His finger pointed towards a queer-looking bearded man dressed in a patchworked *kaftan*; a red *tarbouche* was on his head and he was sitting with a stringed instrument on a rug and posing for photographs for tourists gathered around him. He was even charging a couple of dirhams for it, I could see. I was amused by his picture-perfect presence and his ingenuity.

'Is he for real?' I asked.

'Allah knows! He appeared from somewhere some years back. I always see him here. They call him Qareem Fakir. Harmless fellow!' Zafar announced. I didn't want to miss an opportunity to meet a real fakir, or a subject so photogenic and intriguing, so I went ahead with my camera.

'Twenty dirhams,' he said as soon as he saw me approaching him. I nodded my head and placed the money on his rug.

Contrary to my perception, his voice was unnaturally young for such an attire. His eyes seemed floating and lost, yet there was a boyish twinkle in them as he gathered the notes and obliged the tourists. Occasionally, he smiled. On taking a closer look through my lenses, he appeared much younger than I had anticipated.

That's when I saw an *ektara*. Of course, I recognised it! I had too much Bengali blood running through my veins to miss the symbol of the wandering bards or *bauls* of Bengal. This was going to be interesting, I thought. I had many questions. As we began taking pictures, he eventually started feeling comfortable in my presence and even as the regular crowd of tourists thinned, he stayed seated. It was just the two of us and Zafar left me with a few words.

'Qareem Fakir, do you speak English?' I asked.

'Little bit only,' he replied. The accent caught me completely off guard and I probed: 'Where are you from? How did you get here?'

'I came from the feet of Allah. He brought me here.' Qareem Fakir responded vaguely. I could sense he was reading from a script.

'You are young to be a fakir ...' I said, framing his face on my camera for a portrait.

'Age is an illusion.' He continued his seemingly spiritual staged answers. By now, I had already categorised him as an impostor and was growing curious about his real identity. I wasn't convinced at all that he was a fakir, or that he was a beggar. I had to be patient with my line of queries, I told myself, and continued to take pictures.

'Can you play that instrument for me? I want to take a video. Can I?' I asked.

'Forty dirhams for video,' he said with a smile and picked up the ektara.

As soon as the money landed on his torn brown rug, he started playing the *ektara*.

'Ami ekdino na dekhilam tare. Barir kaache aarshi nogor, shetha porshi boshot kore ...'

(I've never ever seen him in all my days, there's a mystical village near my home, where a certain neighbour lives ...')

'Eta to Lalon Fakir er gaan.' I heard myself announcing that

this was a song by Lalon Fakir.

Qareem Fakir was taken by surprise, but seemingly comforted upon hearing his native tongue spoken in a land so far away from home. This perhaps forced him to drop his disguise. His eyes lit up.

'*Apni Bangali? Lalon zaanen?*' Are you a Bengali? Do you know Lalon? he responded in fluent Bangla, with the accent typical of Bangladesh. The air between us changed with the discovery of a common language. From a suspecting tourist and writer probing into the origins of a fakir in rags, it transformed into an equation where two people from two diverse paths were meeting at a common coordinate and connecting through one language. In a few minutes, he told me that his name was Qareem and that his home town was a small village on the borders of India and Bangladesh. He had grown up listening to *bauls*, and he favoured Lalon. He hadn't thought he would ever become a fakir, because when he ran away from home to a foreign or '*phoren*' country, he didn't realise he would end up as an illegal immigrant in Rome. Or that he would spend a couple of months working as an 'OCDC'.

'OCDC? What is that?' I asked, perplexed.

'Arre, madam, onion-cutter-dish-cleaner! You don't know? That's what they call us.' I could see him chuckling as he shared stories of his struggle for survival in parts of Europe and Africa. 'Those were challenging days, very challenging. I was always running from the police—like a thief—because I had no visa to stay. No one would give me a job without a valid work permit and without a job, I had no money. Sometimes, I did odd jobs but they paid very little. I had no rights.

'By chance, I met another man like me; he was working in

Marrakesh in an Indian restaurant. He helped me escape and brought me along from Rome. I was doing menial jobs first as I stayed with him. I did not have the right papers, you see. Then a few years back, he suddenly died. I had nowhere to go, no permanent job and very little money.

'One day, I just picked up my *ektara* that I had travelled everywhere with and came here to these pink quarters to rest. It's unusually quiet here and the police and security don't bother you. I was so sad and lonely, so I started singing Lalon's songs. Some tourists heard me and paid good money. From then on, this is what I do for a living. Now I charge for everything: whether it is posing for pictures, playing music or letting them take videos. Sometimes, they give me food. I bless them. They call me Qareem Fakir.'

His story captivated me so much that I forgot the passage of time. He asked me if I would like to drink some tea with him. '*Ei shamne ekta Pakistani bhaiyar dokan aase. Onek bhalo cha pawa zaaye. Khaben?*' There's a nice tea shop right across the road run by a Pakistani brother. They make good tea. Do you want some? he said.

I told him that would be great, and that I was happy to pay for both of us. He waved with his hand and walked away briskly. I sat on a pink sandstone plinth next to his soiled and tattered rug, guarding his little treasures—a plastic bottle of water, an aluminium bowl of coins and notes, a red-and-grey chequered cotton kerchief (*gamchha*), the *ektara* that had accompanied him through his troubled days.

By now, Zafar had decided that I was a rather unusual tourist and instead of trailing after me had resorted to parking the car nearby and taking a nap, waiting while I engaged with the queer fakir in a language he didn't understand.

Qareem was back in a while, holding two small glass tumblers of hot masala tea and a loaf of bread. He asked me if I had had lunch, and when I said I had, he politely offered me a glass of tea and sat down on his rug again, biting into the loaf of bread.

'*Aapnar bari kothaye?*' Where is your home?

I told him that my ancestors were zamindars of land hemming the Bengal-Bangladesh border, and while much of the property and wealth could be retained, we lost some during Partition. 'My great-grandfather was a patron of music and played the flute. Spiritualism in our home came in the form of music and musicians—*baul, kirtan*, folk—we didn't have to go to temples to seek divinity,' I explained.

Qareem was so carried away by my lineage to something so close to his own heart that he picked up his *ektara* and started singing again …

'*Barir kaache aarshi nogor, shetha porshi boshot kore.*'

I sat mesmerised, sipping the tea, listening to him singing a soulful *baul* song in the middle of Marrakesh. Music really had no boundaries.

'I have heard from my grandmother that there was once an *ektara* in the family. It used to be a prized possession because it was Lalon Fakir's heirloom,' I shared as he finished his song.

His eyes lit up in surprise.

'It was unique because it had a rose, a pair of folded hands and a star carved on the gourd resonator. As Sufi as it can get. I don't know how my family got it. Anyway, we lost it during Partition, alongside so many other valuable things, including tolerance for other religions and other faiths.' I sighed.

I thought I saw a change in Qareem's expression but dismissed it. I had wasted too much of his time by now so I thanked him for the song and the tea, and offered him some money as baksheesh before getting up to leave.

'Why are you giving me so much money?' he called out.

'Keep it, it may come in handy,' I said as I walked away.

Zafar had parked the car at an arm's length, so I decided to walk to the vehicle, softly humming the song…

'Barir kaache aarshi nogor, shetha porshi boshot kore.'

I heard footsteps following me, and turned around to see Qareem. He was holding the *ektara* in his hand.

'Eita aapni niye zaan'. Please take this with you.

'Maane? Why? Why are you giving it to me? It's your only source of living!'

'Taate ki hoise? Shey ami manage koira nimu.' So what? I can manage without this particular one.

I couldn't understand what he was trying to say or do. The man had nothing to his name but his *ektara* and I could not see why he was giving it away, and to me of all people. He must be mad! Fakirs are hardly normal anyway, I thought! So I said, 'No, thank you' and got into the car. Zafar noticed Qareem coming closer and fearing the worst, started rolling up his sleeves to fight him. I signalled him to stop.

By now, I was seated in the car and Qareem was holding the door, still insisting that I take the *ektara* with me.

'Arre shonen na, eita aapnader zinish. Kemon koira amar kaase soila ashche ami zaanio na. Allah-r ki ase mone shei zaane. Ami to fakir! Ei dekhen!' Listen, this belongs to you. I don't even know how it came to me. Only Allah knows what's on his mind. I am just a fakir. Look!

He turned the *ektara* to the other side, a side that I hadn't seen before, and started rubbing the dust away with his red chequered *gamchha*. From beneath the layers of dust, soil and years of modest living, now appeared a rose, a pair of folded hands and a star.

One Night

In Ward 22, Patient 1136 was unable to sleep. It was lonely in the isolation ward and the silence felt deafening. Rani was the only patient in this makeshift emergency ward. It had been converted from a small community centre into a ward overnight after the pandemic broke out in the region. It was a strange room. Dim yellow lights hung from long iron rods snaking down the roof, and from her bed Rani could only see a part of it. An irregular geometry of wooden planks and iron bars held up the asbestos ceiling. The paint had chipped off the walls in many places, and several gaping spots were without cement too. It exposed the red bricks underneath, the kinds that Rani was used to carrying on her head every day at the construction site. Sometimes she even bore eight of them together, piled up in columns of two over a matted coir cloth.

There were no windows in the ward, at least none that she could see even as she craned her neck. They may have been blocked. The narrow cubicles with their blue fabric partitions separated the cold hospital beds from each other. Her space was just enough for a single bed, a rusty bedside table for medicines and other essentials; only a single medical staff could attend to the patient at a time. Visitors weren't allowed here.

The ward smelled strongly of bleach, and was laced with a nauseating stench from the unclean toilets nearby. It had either been forgotten or completely ignored in a haste to build up the facility. It made Rani want to throw up.

Rani's fever had showed no signs of subsiding for three days despite home medication; her dry coughs had only worsened and every bone in her body ached. She tried drinking a potion of the traditional *kadha* her mother would always prepare with honey, basil and ginger back home whenever she fell sick as a child. It didn't offer much relief. Finally, when she began to feel breathless and fell down unconscious at the construction site where she and her husband worked as daily wage labourers, a pandemonium broke out. The fellow workers raised an alarm and the contractor was forced to call the hospital. An ambulance came through with its blaring sirens in an hour. Raghu, her husband, accompanied her to the nearest hospital.

After a primary interrogation, both Raghu and Rani were asked to clean their hands first with soap and then sanitizer, and given masks to wear. And while Raghu sat on the concrete floor outside the corridor, clueless of what might have struck them, Rani's symptoms were noted with great detail. A lot of whispers were exchanged between the hospital staff. A nurse in protective gear took Rani's body temperature and performed a sudden and painful swab test. Then she was wheeled to another part of the hospital for an emergency test where they also collected her blood sample. Twenty-six-year-old Rani was considered COVID 19 positive. The deadly COVID 19 pandemic had already infected people in over 200 countries and killed more half a million men, women and children across the world.

The ward boy, Jagat Ram, took over as soon as the tests

were done. He belonged to the same community as Rani and knew her well from his village. Pushing her wheelchair, passing by empty corridors and leading her to the back of the hospital, he enquired about her health, and even though she could barely hear his words through her semi-conscious haze, she tried to respond. All she could understand was that she was suspected of a terrible and infectious disease and therefore had to be isolated. She had little idea what that meant. They moved her in a small van to Ward 22, with a nurse and Jagat Ram to accompany her.

It wasn't until evening fell that Dr Manav came to see her, along with the same nurse. He was dressed in a strange outfit that made him look like someone off to space. Rani had seen photographs of people dressed like that, but she had no idea who they were or what they did. Through the mask, Rani could see that he was a pleasant young man. The crow's feet around his eyes wrinkled often as he spoke to Rani, checking on her health. She interpreted that as a smile. He had a moonlike face and two big eyes behind round rimmed glasses. There was nothing remarkable about the way he looked. He was just an average man in his thirties. The only interesting thing may have been the scar on his forehead, right between the brows.

'Are the test results in?' he asked the nurse.

'Not yet, doctor. Maybe later tonight or first thing tomorrow morning. But looks more like a case of normal flu to me.'

'You know we cannot take the risk during these times.'

'Yes, doctor.'

'Good. Then let her rest tonight,' he said to the nurse. He turned to Rani. 'You are not going to be scared sleeping alone here, are you?'

She shook her head weakly. The doctor then asked the nurse

to give Rani some medicines to bring her temperature down and to help her sleep.

'I will see you soon!' he said as he walked out.

Back in the duty officer's room, Dr Manav generously sprayed sanitizer on his hands one more time. Except in the case of an emergency, he was nearly done for the day. These were unprecedented and very tedious days. Times were uncertain and no one quite knew when they would see an end to this pandemic, or even a ray of hope for improvement. The whole world was battling the pandemic and it left everyone, including doctors and healthcare staff, in the lurch every day. Closing the door behind him, Dr Manav took off the many layers of protective gear he had been wearing. It was stifling to breathe through these multi layered clothes, but he had no choice. It was almost summer; the air conditioner still did not work, and the outfit made him feel warm and sweaty. He stripped down to a T-shirt and hung the apron on the hook behind the door.

The duty officer's room was very modestly equipped for a night's rest. There was a small desk with a table lamp, a television and a narrow iron bed that doubled up as a table on which patients were examined.

It was not the kind of bed Dr Manav would like to sleep on, but this makeshift arrangement was way more comfortable than dozing on a chair all night. He was tired and sleepy, yet his mind was restless. He opened a bag and pulled out a small bottle; gulping down the liquid inside in a single go. The spirit burnt his throat, but he liked the sensation it left behind. For those who lectured him about not drinking while on duty, he smirked a bit: 'These are extraordinary times, so extraordinary behaviour is permissible.'

He turned on the television, but he could not concentrate on anything that was being broadcast. The news channels were either debating or presenting more data on the pandemic; death tolls were only growing. He thought about his parents and how they wanted him to get married this year. 'It wouldn't happen with the virus in the air. I may die a bachelor, Ma,' he joked much to her chagrin during his last call home. Women are just so naïve, he thought. Either they overreact or they don't get it. He immediately thought of Rani. That woman has no clue if she has the virus or not, and that she could die tomorrow. Such a sultry beauty. What a waste!' he muttered to himself as he raised the bottle again and poured some more liquid down his throat.

He was indifferently surfing through the channels when someone knocked on his door. He hid the bottle back in his bag and opened the door. It was Jagat Ram, the ward boy.

'Sir, patient number 1142 is making a lot of noise. The old man first eats hospital food for free, then he finishes the food his wife brings for him, and then complains of acidity and gas! Now, he says that he cannot sleep because his stomach is bloated. If you eat so much, what will the poor stomach do? He is making so much noise that other patients cannot sleep in the same ward. Shall we give him some antacid or a sedative? And patient 1129 will be discharged tomorrow morning. The other doctor said he can go home. We need your signature for the early discharge, and sir, patient 1136, her report has just come. Nurse told me to show it to you.'

'Wait, wait!' Manav scratched his head. 'Who is patient 1136? Jagat Ram, how many times do I have to tell you I cannot remember numbers like that. Do you even know how many patients I see every day? How will I identify them using numbers? Give me some references to the case. What report are you talking about?'

'Sorry, sir! I am reading from the register. Patient 1136 is that girl, sir. The one from my village. The one in the isolation ward. Her report has come. Here, sir,' Jagat Ram pulled out a sheet of paper from the ream he was carrying.

Dr Manav signed off the other papers and took a close look at the report. Negative, it said. Phew! He heaved a sigh of relief.

Just then, his phone buzzed with a text. It was Rajat from school. 'Hey mate! Wassup?'

'Nothing much. Just another night shift,' he responded after Jagat Ram left.

'At least you are alive! What are you doing?'

'Twiddling my thumbs! On duty. Moron! What else can I do in a hospital?'

'I didn't ask you to study medicine. No hot patients?'

'Naah!' he lied.

'No virus yet, I hope?'

'Not yet! Touchwood. There was a suspect. A young woman. She was reported negative.'

'That's some luck. Is *she* hot?'

'She is a migrant worker, dude.'

'That doesn't answer my question. Is she hot?'

'Yes, kinda! Sultry.'

'So, that poor babe isn't so poor after all. She is also corona-free.'

'So what?'

'You will die a virgin, bro.' Rajat sent a laughing emoji, mocking him further.

'I gotta go back to work. Speak later. Cheers,' Dr Manav texted back and silenced his phone. It was almost close to midnight; this was his last night duty for the week. The stress and anxiety had started taking its toll on his body and mind.

I probably need some fresh air, he thought and stepped out of his room. He walked into the ward for a last round, called Jagat Ram and told him that he was going out for a few minutes. 'Extraordinary times permit extraordinary behaviour,' he repeated to himself and went straight up to Ward 22.

In the darkness of the night, even as the dim yellow lights hung their heads over the cubicles separated by thick blue, the modesty of a woman was outraged by her own doctor. Through the haze of medication and sleep, Rani, trapped alone in an isolation ward far away from the din of the hospital, was gagged and raped several times that night, until she started to bleed excessively. She didn't know who the perpetrator was; only she noticed a scar on his forehead in the middle of his eyebrows. She gave in. What else could she have done! She was alone, young, too weak to fight and of course, 'corona-free' as Dr Manav's friend had said. They found her dead the next morning, lying in a pool of blood. Her husband, Raghu was told that it was 'death due to internal bleeding'.

That evening, Jagat Ram was sitting quietly outside the duty officer's room, crushing some tobacco in his palm. He was deeply saddened by Rani's sudden death. Such a lovely young girl!

'God knows what was in that report, she bled overnight and died!' he wondered.

'Jagat Ram!' the nurse called in haste.

'Yes, yes sister?'

'That patient…'

'Which one?'

'Arre that girl from your community. The one who died this morning.' Her voice was anxious.

'Yes, Rani. What about her?'

'Did you see the report?'

'No, sister. I gave it to Doctor sahab last night.'

'Oh no! You already gave it to him? There was a mistake. Now, Dr Manav will scold me for mixing things up. We did another test with her blood sample and she is definitely coronavirus positive in that report. Poor girl …!'

She muttered to herself. 'Never knew internal bleeding could occur in such cases. God only knows what the symptoms and treatment are. Everything is a presumption now. Learning new things everyday with this pandemic, aren't we? Now we have to call the authorities. She can't be cremated like everyone else, can she? Oh my God! Her husband must have gotten it too. You know him, right? We have to test him too!' She was rambling in a panic. Jagat was still trying to understand what all this meant. The nurse continued, 'Anyway, since you handled her, be careful, okay? You should get a test done as well. I will tell Dr Manav too …'

The Judgement Call

Corporate Headquarters, Heaven

From an outsider's perspective, it is business as usual in the corporate headquarters of Heaven. If you thought those who made their way in had access to *hoor*s, *pari*s and *apsara*s, wore silken robes and lived like kings without moving their butts … rein your imagination in!

We are talking about Heaven.

This isn't some fancy dress competition or a set from Bollywood. People work hard and are *dying* to get entry here, and they work harder to ensure that their roles don't become redundant or outsourced amidst restructuring and transformations; they 'live' well by partying hard after a long day's work. That's the only time you see the fancy bits, the props and eye candies. It's just a teeny-weeny piece of the full mosaic, not the whole tile. Get real!

However, if an insider's lead can be taken seriously, God has apparently announced a breakthrough strategy. It has all of Heaven busy with implementing the 'game plan for success 10.0. GPS', that is what they call it. Some dead ad guru coined it. Don't ask where he did that! Infinity perhaps. As a founder and CEO, God here multitasks and wears many hats. He has to; He is so consumed by His own autonomy! This isn't the kind of role you can delegate, you see. Plus, He is a control freak. He just has to be everywhere, doing everything. Therefore, the onus of people management (yes, even after death) also lies on him. He has a team of smart intellectuals to offer consultations, but we also know, unfortunately, not many HR personnel end up in Heaven after being told to 'Go to hell' so often by almost all their employees. Oh well!

God, according to reliable sources, has been influenced by the openness of a few democracies, and has fairly decided to launch a new grievance cell near the doors to Heaven.

'We are an equal opportunity organisation and believe in open, two-way communication,' the position statement from Heaven said. It went on to add, 'So, before we dedicate our resources to the various verticals of our structure, where we would allocate Hell or Heaven to accommodate you or recycle you back to the world for another tenure, we want to hear from each one of you. We want 360-degree feedback on what had worked, what didn't, the prayers and appeals that were heard, ignored or acted upon. This is the only way we can improve our operational excellence whilst also being transparent about setting our expectations, performance management system, appraisal and ratings.'

A rejoinder clarified: 'All our bonuses are in kind. No monetary transactions are allowed here.' The leadership team that spearheads the drive on sustainable cost management is particularly relieved to see this disclaimer.

To ensure people do not mistake the grievance cell for a concierge and let it deviate into the habitual fine art of service entitlement, God has also been particularly keen on a brand identity. He has ordered for a new logo but it looks like a disfigured elephant's ear. It is also in shining neon. His trusted accountant, Chitragupta, who has been single-handedly managing logistics and administration for all new entrants since the beginning of time, has been assigned the new role of co-managing this first port of entry beyond life. God, however, wants to lead this new 'innovative, people-friendly' initiative himself. He is supported by a strong team of steerco with Urvashi, the brand ambassador of Heaven, Yama, the dark face of Hell and a certain podgy man with yellow hair and a distorted facial expression to represent the living world. The team is well represented, Chitragupta thinks. After all, inclusion and diversity must start, or end, here.

But He is exasperated even before the queue outside starts to check in. Menaka, who is supposed to manage the reception, has called in sick. Argh! This is her fifth unwarranted leave this month.

'Must be a hangover from last night's party. After her scandalous past, this woman still has not learnt her lesson,' Chitragupta broods. But now, He must find a solution. These eleventh-hour crises never go away, not even for God, not even in the headquarters of Heaven. This is not how he had planned for Day 1 to begin. He looks at his team and wonders who should be manning the reception now that Menaka has let him down. He measures the two men from Hell and Earth, assesses whether their faces match those of a quintessential receptionist, quickly dismisses the thought, and finally asks Urvashi to step in and help him.

'Urvashi, I need something done quickly. Can you please cover for Menaka and help me with the registration at the reception? Many thanks in advance.' He sends this out to her. In other words, move your butt and obey. No is not an option.

Urvashi protests, 'Hey, I have enough on my plate, and I don't have the bandwidth—'

Her words fall on deaf ears as Chitragupta is already out of the door, busy with headcounts. Urvashi, although forever keen to help, grudgingly looks at her own to-do list for the day and takes the seat at the reception. 'No one listens to anyone here. What's this charade about the grievance cell about anyway? she mutters to herself.

Outside the door, which should rightfully be called a gate, for it is the largest ever unscalable, unmanned gate beyond life, stands a teeming crowd of impatient humans. Men, women and children, bustling with energy as if they have all won the golden ticket to Willy Wonka's chocolate factory. They are, of course, clueless who will be judged first. Amongst all living beings, only humans are judged based on their performance. Plants and animals have a 'green' corridor to heaven. It sounds a bit biased, and some may argue that the rules must be the same for all, but that's just how it is, and one should be ready to die knowing this.

To avoid chaos, Urvashi takes charge of the public announcement system: 'Ladies and gentlemen, boys and girls. Our door to Heaven, Hell and Earth will open in a few minutes. Please come to the reception for registration and verification and head straight to the grievance cell for your personal interviews. Thank you for your patience. We will now call you by your names and place of death.'

A loud buzz breaks out among the queues as people shuffle between lines and argue over who goes first.

'Is there a separate queue for priority check-in? I can't be with the cattle class, you see,' a man in a business suit with a gold wristlet shouts out.

'Isn't there a special queue for women? No line for women? You are expecting me to stand with these thousand men? What if someone tries to molest me? What about my security?' cries out a once-well-known social activist.

'Anything for senior citizens?' says a feeble voice behind her. A little child wails in despair, adding to the demands.

Bimboboti, waiting all this while with her shiny coolers over her head, fans her face and takes her smartphone out. She swipes to her camera and checks her usual pout. The waterproof lipstick, even after drowning, hasn't smudged. The brand had claimed well. It's all good for her, but there is no signal and the battery is dying! Darn, how can she take her selfie at the door of Heaven for an Instagram post?

Grievance Cell

Chitragupta adjusts his seat as Urvashi directs the first candidate of the day to the grievance cell. A fiery, middle-aged woman walks in. She is dressed in a cotton saree with a broad border, her hair is neatly tied in a bun and she has a glowing red dot in the centre of her forehead. Before Chitragupta can measure her up, she adjusts her spectacles and gauges him instead—up and down. Her authoritative look intimidates him a bit.

'Madam, as you know, we have just launched this new programme, where we want to be listening—'

'Listening?' she interrupts sharply. 'You never heard anything when I appealed and shouted for your attention whilst I was down there fighting for social issues and women's rights, protesting against governments and authority. Never supported my cause while I was alive. Instead, you let those goons kill me! What will I do with your listening now?'

Chitragupta hadn't prepared for this. 'I understand, madam. Not all your prayers may have been answered. But we are trying to discuss it with you. We can look into the matter together and see how we can come to a mutual agreement based on your performance as a human in your lifetime ...' Chitragupta tries to explain in vain.

'Get a better hearing machine. Clearly, nothing is getting into your ears. Listen, I don't care about what you want to discuss. I have had a long day, and after the hunger strike that was under way before those buggers bashed my head in, I am famished. Really! Now that I am dead anyway, all I care about is a good meal and a clean bed. You put me through to Heaven right now. I spent all my life working for social causes and doing community service. I am entitled to Heaven,' she argues in a commanding tone.

'Madam, no one is entitled to Heaven—' Chitragupta tries to negotiate.

'Oh, don't give me that crap. I know how these things work. Call your boss. Call your supervisor. I want to talk to him. I am not moving an inch from here unless you promise me a seat in Heaven.'

Chitragupta, now under pressure rushes to God and shares a quick note on the *bawaal* or pandemonium the activist was creating. They agree that it's best to shut her up by giving her what she wants. Better that than letting her influence her peers.

Chitragupta comes back with a smile. 'Madam, I have

made a special recommendation for you, and using His most discretionary power, my boss has agreed to give your case a consideration. You will be granted access to Heaven for three months on probation first—'

'What probation? This is not a temporary arrangement. I want a permanent seat.' She isn't willing to give up so easily.

'It is just a formality, madam. Once in probation, you can be sure that your role will become permanent. Congratulations, madam,' says Chitragupta.

Assured by this she softens. 'Thank you.' She looks happy now. 'Oh, please tell them that I am a vegan. So, they must arrange for me accordingly.' Urvashi comes to receive the lady and as they walk out, he hears them speak.

'You can wear these clothes freely here? No one makes a passing comment or attempts to molest you? Let me know if anyone ever teases you. I led a "me-too" campaign back home.'

'Next!' Chitragupta calls out, wiping off a droplet of sweat.

The man who walks in through the door has a *Main hoon Don* air about him. Dressed in a white linen shirt and blue denim, a ponytail and an earring, he carries the Latino-bartender-turned-mafia stereotype with much élan.

Chitragupta can smell the tobacco and alcohol even as this candidate takes a seat. 'The incorrigible idiot died of cancer, yet he won't learn,' he thinks. He clears his throat and explains the objectives behind the grievance cell.

'Hey man, I don't have any grievances. I got everything I wanted in life. I didn't have to ask for anyone's help. I was a self-made man. I made money, big time! I was an entertainer. Fame, money, success and fans followed me wherever I went. I was a go-getter,' the don boasts.

'I see, but you have also invested a lot of that money into drugs, buying guns, funding underworld activities and if I were to follow rumours, running a drug mafia in Cartagena.' Chitragupta says, looking through the files. He doesn't like this man. 'This is a model case for Hell. What's the point of this charade?' he grumbles silently to himself.

'Huh ... so what? I can do whatever I want to with my money. I didn't force anyone to take drugs. If they had it, it was their choice. I sold guns, but guns bought by some people killed other people. It was not me. I didn't kill them,' the man argues.

'What about all the innocent women you have cheated?'

'Oh, I was just popular with women. They couldn't resist me.' The man starts to laugh, showing off a nicotine-stained set of dentures. Chitragupta's patience is beginning to wear thin. He wants to close this discussion and move on right away. 'Okay, let's be clear on this. You are going to Hell.'

The man seems aghast. He tries to put forward an argument again. 'What? I was a star, rich and famous. I have the licence to do things differently.'

'You may have been an artist and talented in your own ways, you may have been a great success at work, and you may have even made a name for yourself. You may have looked like a million bucks and gathered a few fans, but at the end of the day, I will still judge you, and judge I will, only on one parameter ... were you a good human? And by that measure, you were a mess caught in your own web of lies, megalomania and narcissism. Everyone else was an option for you to get richer and more famous. You always put your selfish needs first, irrespective of what the consequences could be for anyone else. That's irresponsible. Sorry, gentleman, but Hell it is for you,'

Chitragupta's voice is now firm.

Yama, at the sound of Hell, emerges from his diabolic den to lend a hand to the don. He is used to being rough with these rogues. 'They don't deserve any better.' He laughs unapologetically. The man protests at first, and then gives in with a wink. He cannot possibly die twice.

'Next!' Chitragupta calls out.

A frightened, nervous little girl limps in. She must be about eight or nine. Her eyes are pools of anguish and hurt. Her clothes are tainted in blood; a big clot has dried on her head. Her nails are black and broken. There are blue and red marks on her arms and fingers. Chitragupta rushes to ask her if she is in pain but the child doesn't speak. Chitragupta tries to comfort her by offering her water. Her weak hands tremble as she folds them in a gesture, as if begging for mercy. There's a heart-wrenching blankness in her eyes. It is as if life itself has been erased from her soul. A confused Chitragupta asks God to intervene.

'I am God. You don't have to fear anyone here. Tell me if you have any grievances. I can take appropriate actions.'

She still doesn't speak. 'Her body looks like it has been tortured by beasts. Chitragupta, read out her record. Why is she here? What is her story?' God asks his trusted employee.

'Asifa Bano went missing on 10 January, 2018. Her family of Gujjars were living in a village around 70 km east of Jammu. On that afternoon, her mother recalls, Asifa went to the forest to bring home their horses. The horses returned, but Asifa did not. The worried parents and some neighbours started looking for her. Armed with flashlights, lanterns and axes, they went deep into the forest and searched through the night. But they could not find her. Complaining to the police did not help either. Five days later, Asifa's body was found. She had been tortured. According to the investigators, Asifa was confined in a local temple for several days and given sedatives that had kept her unconscious. The charge sheet alleges that she was "raped for days, tortured and then finally murdered". She was strangled to death and then hit on the head twice with a stone.' Chitragupta's voice chokes as he reads from the file.

'She was raped and killed in a temple?' God trembles in rage at the thought.

'Yes, my Lord,' Chitragupta confirms.

'Why was I not notified? Were her prayers, her cries for mercy so weak? How could I not know of this?' God's head hangs in shame.

Asifa, clueless of the difference between Hell and Earth for she hasn't seen either, quietly sits listening to the discussion and thinks of her home in Kashmir ... of her Ammi, Abbu, her friends and her beloved horses.

God kneels down to look Asifa in the eye. He holds her broken soul in his embrace and asks for forgiveness from the innocent little soul. To Chitragupta, he says, 'She is not going anywhere. She is staying with me from now on.'

'Next,' Chitragupta calls out. His voice is trembling.

Bimboboti is restless. She has been waiting too long and the absence of a Wi-Fi connection bores her. What a freaky day this had been! First, she lost her balance and breath after being swept off by a giant wave, just as she was posing with her best pout for a selfie with her latest boyfriend on their dream holiday. Two, that rascal turned out to be a good swimmer and survived, while she had to say goodbye forever to her happening life. She feels like her death is wasted.

She is full of grievances and she summarises them as she steps into the cell. She strides in as if she's walking on the ramp and then, with her left hand on the hip, poses like the quintessential dancing girl of Harappa. 'Listen, whoever you are, there must be some mistake. Look at me, I am so young and beautiful. How can I die so early? I have never harmed anyone, nor have I thought of anyone with evil intent. Actually, to be honest, I don't even know many people personally.'

'But you have some 30,000 followers on Instagram,' Chitragupta is surprised by her confidence.

'Those are followers. It's just timepass. They are not real friends or people. I haven't even had a steady boyfriend. There are so many places I am yet to see, so many things to do. I haven't even started. I have never been fully happy, nor rich. I am way too young to die like this! How can you kill me so early?'

'Oh, but on your social media everything looks perfect. You look like a been-there-done-that individual.' Chitragupta tries to understand.

'But that's posing, no? Not real,' she explains.

'What do you mean?' He scrolls as he speaks. 'Did you not go on that holiday to St Moritz? Did your friends not come for your birthday party? Did you not eat all those fancy meals? There are albums after albums! How can it be just posing? How can you complain of an incomplete life? This is all so self-contradictory!'

'Argh, you don't understand. I did go on that holiday, but I didn't see anything. My friends came over for my birthday dinner, but we didn't talk much; and frankly, I can't even remember how the food tasted. I was busy posing for the pictures, no?'

'So, in short, nothing about your life felt real.'

'Yes, in a way. I was not living those moments. I was just capturing them.'

'Who's at fault then?'

'I don't know! But if I go to Heaven or Hell now, I won't see anything ever again.' Her voice sounds sad but she does not break. Chitragupta's, however, softens. 'Will you live any differently if you were reborn?'

'I cannot promise, but I will try,' Bimboboti says.

'Fair enough, I will grant you another tenure only on one condition. You will value every moment and every human connection in your life. You must pause and notice the world around you, live for yourself and not for the gallery. In the middle of a beautiful moment, if you want to capture it, go ahead. Don't fake a moment just to post it on social media. It's so misleading. For you, and for us.' Chitragupta smiles as he lays down the rules. Bimboboti is ecstatic! She throws her slender arms around Chitragupta, hugging him and thanking him for another life.

Urvashi is done until the lunch break. It's been a busy Day 1. The grievance cell seems like a successful idea. At least, people now know how judgement calls are made after death, and why they must use their judgement when they are alive. From Chitragupta's new cell, she can hear Bimboboti's excited voice and part of the conversation.

'Thank you, thank you, thank you! Do you have a phone?'

'Yes, I do.'

'Can we click a selfie?'

'What?'

'Just kidding!' She breaks into a fit of giggles.

Of Stars, Planets and Boundaries

'There's someone beyond you and me. Someone who sits high up there, watching and controlling every movement of our lives. There is somebody we haven't seen, cannot touch, hear or smell, but you know, he's present, and like a seasoned chess grandmaster, he knows it all. Every single move and the repercussion of each—good, bad and ugly—he has a catalogue of a million permutations and combinations. He knows every game; played, lost and won! Past, present and future, everything is predetermined,' Jonathan said reflectively, looking at the vast expanse of the greenish-blue Atlantic Ocean in front of him. His posture was yogic and his voice was laden with a deep-seated spirituality. What's more, he was not addressing a finite audience, but only speaking to the boundless sequence of ocean waves lashing upon the rocky bed bordering the Cape of Good Hope in South Africa.

I was drawn to this unusual spectacle of a man sitting all by himself, facing the limitless blue ocean, all whilst a pride of ostriches walked around him on such a beautiful spring afternoon. The birds did not distract or disturb him.

I had found these coordinates on my drive back from visiting a lighthouse on the tip of the southernmost piece of land in the African continent. It was my first trip to Cape Aghulas. Driving past the scene, my primary notion was to stop the car and capture the moment on camera. I stepped out of the car and began walking towards him, trying not to disturb the man who seemed to be in a trance.

However, Jonathan spotted my unstable footsteps over the slippery rocks and waved to me with a welcoming smile. It was almost as if he were waiting for someone to break his meditation.

'Hi there! Sorry if I disturbed you,' I said apologetically. The rocks were slimy and a few of them were covered with thick slush. I wondered why someone would walk through this undulating wet ground to choose a seat at the far end of it.

'That's all right. I wasn't doing much,' he responded gently.

'I thought you were meditating. Looked a bit like yoga,' I said, noticing that he was sitting in the lotus position.

'Haha … yes, you could say that. Yoga, it is, young lady!' His voice was deep and his diction was clear. He must have been in his late fifties and he had a part-Asian, part-European face. He was suntanned and his eyes were like pools of green, but his clothes were ordinary khakis and a bit soiled. I must admit, I struggled to gauge his origin.

'In case you are wondering where I learnt that from, I must tell you that I spent a lot of time in Asia.' He seemed to have read my mind. 'My name is Jonathan. And you, are you Indian or Pakistani?'

'Indian by birth, but I live in Singapore.' I found myself standing next to him, admiring the beauty and vastness of the Atlantic in front of us.

'Aha, Singapore? That's a fine city, as they say.' He signalled me to sit down on a rock beside him.

A small pride of brown ostriches were marching in front of us. They seemed unperturbed by human presence. I grabbed my camera, pulled the sling bag across my shoulders and sat down next to Jonathan. The rock was damp, but I couldn't care about keeping my clothes dry when I was literally sitting on the edge of a continent. In the distance, I could see the white outline of another land mass. I put my eye through the viewfinder and tried to zoom in on the lens. I thought I saw whales in the far lining of the blue.

'Are you a photographer?'

'Not quite. I just capture moments and then tell their stories.' I smiled.

'Aha, so you are a storyteller? A writer or a journalist?'

'Well, I am a bit of both,' I responded, looking at the sparkle of sunshine-soaked water droplets dancing over the waves. I explained that I had spent twelve years of my career as a journalist, and that I had also published a book of short stories not too long ago.

'Do people still read books?' he asked bluntly.

'Not many do, but some really kind and curious ones venture into it. For the most part, authors are a forgotten tribe,' I replied.

He smiled at my honesty and added, 'You see, I don't read newspapers or books any more. So if you are a celebrated author or something, I would not know.'

There was no such risk, I convinced him.

'You tell me, how did you end up here? There is no habitation around,' I said, looking at the landscape around us, wanting to change the topic. He was my object of interest. I didn't want the focus to shift to me. For as far as my eyes could see, I could only see yellow protea and other bushy shrubs around the rocky cliffs. I spotted two baboons sitting gleefully on a milestone on the road, biting into the yellow flowers and spitting out what they did not like. There was no sign of people.

'I was looking for peace and I have found it here. We all look for something, don't we? We don't rest till we have found it,' he said, turning his eyes away from mine.

'Yes, that's true,' I agreed, but desiring to know more, I egged him on. But why here? This isn't the kind of place where you could find the Dalai Lama. It's so remote, and so far from humanity.'

'That's what makes it special. I don't like being with humans any more. Here, there are these baboons and ostriches, the ocean and me. I live by my own, on my own and even if it sounds selfish, for my own. Over the years, I have begun to enjoy my own company more than anyone else's.'

'Do you ever feel lonely?'

'No. If you are lonely when you are alone, you are in bad company, young lady.' He laughed heartily.

I joined him in the laughter and agreed, 'Well said, Jonathan. There's something therapeutic about being self-content.'

'It is healing. Since you are a writer, let me tell you a story. How much time do you have?'

'Oh, all the time in the world for a story,' I responded immediately, putting my camera aside and pulling out a pack of potato crisps and a bottle of water from my bag. He reacted to my childlike enthusiasm with a smile.

'Once upon a time, long ago in Saigon, there lived a young man. He was half-American, half-Vietnamese by birth, thanks to an American soldier who had impregnated a Saigonese girl and later died during the American War in 1975. Their young son was a happy and carefree soul and made an honest living as a tour guide. He also drove a taxi through the busiest streets of Saigon. His American appearance attracted foreign tourists and his familiarity with the locals gave him a competitive advantage. Every morning, he would pick up tourists and businessmen from the grand Hotel Majestic, situated on the corner of Dong Khoi and Ton Duc Thang Street, and would take them around the bustling alleys of Saigon.'

After setting the backdrop to his story, he stopped to look at me.

'It's an interesting location. I have been to Ho Chi Minh City and found it very intriguing, very quaint and very mysterious,' I remarked.

'Yes, it is,' he agreed and continued. 'Amongst his many passengers, there were a few who liked him for his jovial disposition, knew him by name and would specifically ask the hotel concierge for his services. One of his old clients was an old Chinese silk magnate, Mr Edmund Tan.

'Mr Tan was a well-known businessman in Saigon. He imported silks from China. There were rumours in the market, however, that he also dealt in firearms and had made his fortune as an arms dealer during the American War. The young man soon discovered that the reason for his frequent visits to Saigon were more than business; he had a beautiful young Vietnamese mistress who lived in Saigon's infamous District 1. Many a night he had to drive past a maze of brothels where "butterflies of the night" lined up to offer services, amidst rows of dimly lit strip clubs, bars and massage parlours, to drop the illustrious Mr Tan at the doorstep of a modest two-storey house. He had to pick him up in the early hours of the morning from the same address.'

'Did he ever get to see the mistress?' I asked curiously.

'Only on two occasions. Both times, she came to the balcony as the car was driving away. She was like an empty oyster shell, strikingly beautiful yet without a pearl.'

'That's a melancholic description.' I could not resist the intervention. It seemed like he could almost picture her as he retold the story.

'Hmm.' His voice was controlled.

'Okay. Then?'

'Then, one rainy night, as this young man was dropping Mr Tan at his usual destination, the old silk tycoon paid him a heavy tip and asked him to come very early the next morning. The young man arrived in good time for his customer, saw a glimpse of the lady at the balcony and began to drive through a thick cloud of winter fog.

"Take me to the airport. Drive as fast as you can. I have a flight to catch," Mr Tan ordered from the backseat. Though visibility was significantly compromised because of the thick blanket of morning mist, the young man manoeuvred through empty by-lanes at dawn quickly. Suddenly, from nowhere came a young boy in a moped, right in front of his speeding taxi! It all happened in a wink. The taxi driver barely had the time to press the brakes or manipulate the steering wheel before he saw that the moped was badly hit. He did see the young body of the boy as it flew across the street. His taxi came to a screeching halt in another thirty seconds, but by then it was too late. The lifeless body of the young boy was lying in a pool of blood on the side of the road. The damaged moped could be seen at a distance.'

'Oh my God! How gruesome! What happened then? Was he arrested? Did anyone see?'

'No, before anyone could come out of their homes, Mr Tan ordered the cabbie to get back to his seat and they sped away. The fog provided good cover for the escape.'

'What? They left the dead boy on the street! How cruel and irresponsible!' I was invested in his story and had begun to seethe with anger.

'Yes, unfortunately so! Mr Tan was too grand a man to be caught in a hit-and-run case, especially in the red-light district of the town. A police case would have opened up a Pandora's box for him; his reputation would have been at stake. The poor young cabbie, on the other hand, though guilty as hell, had no other option but to run from the site and escape the eyes of the law. Had he surrendered he would have been the one arrested for the death of the boy. He had no money to hire a lawyer, nor did he have connections to prove that it was an accident. Any imprisonment would have simply meant losing a life and a living.' Jonathan paused here and looked thoughtfully at the ocean.

'But it was wrong. Did the young cabbie ever find out who that young boy on the moped was?'

'You seem to be reading my mind,' Jonathan responded, returning to his story. 'Yes, the guilt of having killed an innocent boy forced him to go back to the red-light district. He could not eat, sleep or breathe in peace without knowing if the child had really died, and if he had a family. So he kept going there, hoping to find the truth whilst his conscience lived with the harshness of his crime.'

'Isn't it generally criminal psychology to come back and

revisit the scene of the crime?' I inquired.

'Yes, you could say that, but this man was not a criminal. He had the blood of a young boy on his hands, but it had been an accident! And accidents happen without motive. They can happen to anyone, any time,' Jonathan sounded defensive.

'What about running away from responsibility? That's not an accident, that's inhumane and immoral,' I argued.

'Not everything is so black and white.'

'Fair enough, then what happened?' I was growing restless. This could not simply be a story about a hit-and-run case in a red-light district in Saigon, I thought. There must be more.

'Well, for a while everything was very quiet. The young cabbie continued with his life and eventually found out that the boy had indeed died. The deceased used to deliver newspapers and support his mother, a prostitute, with her meagre earnings near where he was killed. He had a younger brother who now did the same job every morning. Mr Tan did not visit Saigon for almost a year, or if he did, he chose to stay in another hotel and not Hotel Majestic. The young cabbie was not summoned again.

'Then one day, he came back to Hotel Majestic and asked the concierge for the same cabbie. He wanted to go to the same place that night. There was no sense of remorse or acknowledgment of what had transpired on his last trip. His sharp eyes were cold and distant, and for the first time, the cabbie wished he could refuse this customer.'

'Why didn't he?' I asked impatiently.

'It is because he was poor. How could he refuse a customer who paid him such heavy tips?' Jonathan continued. 'So, on yet another winter night, the cabbie drove past a maze of brothels where "butterflies of the night" lined up to offer service, amidst rows of dimly lit strip clubs, bars and massage parlours to drop the illustrious Mr Tan at the doorstep of a modest two-storey house and agreed to pick him up in the early hours of the next morning. Like *deja-vu*, the mistress who looked like a barren oyster shell came out of the shadows and stood at the balcony. Once again, they drove through a tunnel of fog, bypassing the thin early morning traffic in the alleys, and then a young boy with reams of newspapers on a moped collided with the taxi. The cabbie spotted the mangled moped and the injured young boy in a pool of blood lying by the kerbside. Mr Tan was heard grumbling, hurling abuses, when the cabbie brought the young boy into the back seat of the car. They broke into an angry argument until the cabbie pushed Mr Tan out of his car and drove the boy to the nearest hospital. Unfortunately, they declared him dead.'

'Oh no! Then? What happened to the cabbie?' I asked, somewhat relieved that the story had a conscience.

'He surrendered to the police and served a sentence: imprisonment for seven years.' Jonathan's voice was soft.

'And Mr Tan? Did he own up?'

'Haha … no! The Mr Tans of the world never own up. He was a big man, and even though some mud was flung upon his name, he used all his connections and escaped unscathed.'

'A true criminal. Did the cabbie find out who this boy was?'

'Yes, he did. The boy was the younger brother of the newspaper boy who had been killed a year back.'

'But this is incredible! Two brothers died exactly in the same way at the hand of the same cabbie, and with the same passenger in the back seat. How can there be such a coincidence?' I felt sympathetic towards the poor and punished cab driver. 'Do you know where he is now?'

Instead of responding, Jonathan took a bite of a potato crisp and drank some water from my bottle. He handed the bottle back to me, shook my hands and stood up.

'Do you believe in stars and planets controlling and setting boundaries in your life? I don't, but I know, for sure, that there's someone beyond you and me who sits high up there, watches and controls every movement in our lives. There is somebody we haven't seen, cannot touch, hear or smell. But you know he's present and like a seasoned chess grandmaster, he knows it all ...'

'... everything is predetermined.' With those words echoing in my ears, he walked away, smoothly gliding over the slippery rock bed, across to the meandering road to where his tall frame became a small dot against the horizon.

Note

In July 1975, Erskine Lawrence Ebbin, a seventeen-year-old inhabitant of the Bermuda Islands, was riding along the road on his moped when he was hit by a taxi. Almost a year prior, also in July, Erskine's brother—who was also seventeen—was killed. He was riding the same moped and he was killed in a taxi accident as well. Behind the wheel was the same driver and he was carrying the same passenger.

Acknowledgements

Every day, I wake up and make a plan to be happy. I do all kinds of things to indulge myself: I write a poem, I buy a book, I shop for my family, I plan a holiday, I cook a meal that my family enjoys, I call my parents, I connect with friends, I read old letters from my daughter, I play with my dog, I discover an old song and dance and sing a tra-la-la in the rain and the shower, I laugh without inhibitions, cracking the stupidest joke at my own expense. I take the greatest pride in my achievements and I forgive myself for all my blunders. Every day, I wake up with a simple plan to be happy and life has been good so far.

I am indebted to all who partake in this simple everyday routine, who take a moment to pause with me and to inspire my stories, either by sharing what's intrinsic to them or by sharing their priceless gems they cannot let go of. Either way, with you I count my abundant treasures—acquired and destined.

I would like to acknowledge the enormous support I have been given to make *An Unborn Desire* possible. My sincerest gratitude to my family and my friends who have listened to my sudden outbursts of spontaneous emotions, motivated me to put them into words, read and reread several versions of my drafts without protest. I am particularly grateful to my dearest friend, Sushmita Das, for all the stimulating chats, detailed analyses and long discussions on everything under the sun over our favourite carrot cakes and afternoon tea, many of which have prompted me to write a story. A million thanks to my forever friend, Farzana Mayesha, for always thinking of my well-being, including her recommendations for finding a writing table so that the book doesn't become a backbreaking experience. I must thank my husband, Dr Swarup Mukherjee, my sister, Sukanya and my mentor, MD Ramesh, for their honest feedback, unconditional confidence and unflinching support.

I am immensely grateful to my editor, Dr Bina Biswas, for trusting me as an author, seeing the value in my endeavours to capture those invaluable moments of learning and sharing, and bringing these characters and events to life through my writing.

And last, but not the least, I remain perpetually grateful to my parents for all their blessings all the time.

Shukraan.